Body Count

Netra Antionette

Netra Antionette

Body Count

Copyright © 2025 by Netra Antionette

All rights reserved.

No part of this book may be reproduced, distributed, or transmitted in any form or by any means, including photocopying, recording, or other electronic or mechanical methods, without the prior written permission of the publisher. This is a work of fiction. Names, characters, places, events, and incidents are either products of the author's imagination or used fictitiously. Any resemblance to actual persons, living or dead, or actual events is purely coincidental.

Edited by Markd by Tylee

Cover design by Netra Antionette

ISBN: 979-8-9985771-1-6

Requests for permission should be addressed to: Netra Antionette

via the contact form at www.netraantionette.com/contact

Contents

Dedication	V
Author's Note	VI
Trigger Warnings	VIII
Playlist	X
1. Rivah	1
2. Rivah	7
3. Rivah	18
4. Rivah	28
5. Kross	41
6. Rivah	51
7. Kross	58
8. Rivah	64
9. Kross	70
10. Rivah	75
11. Kross	86
12. Rivah	93
13. Kross	103
14. Rivah	109
15. Kross	116

16.	Rivah	120
17.	Kross	129
18.	Rivah	139
19.	Kross	146
20.	Rivah	153
21.	Kross	160
22.	Rivah	165
23.	Rivah	171
24.	Epilogue	177
	Netra's Notebook	184

Dedication

Your body is never a battleground for their approval.
It's your playground. Your damn masterpiece. Your story to write —
and you don't owe a single soul an explanation for how you heal, explore, or bloom
Let them talk. Let them choke on their assumptions.
Let them call it a body count when really? It's just receipts of your freedom.
Because you were made to be wild, to be wanted, to be worshipped on your own damn terms.
Soft when you feel like it. Savage when you need to be.
And always, unapologetically yours.
Because your worth was never between your legs — it was always between your ears and behind your ribcage.

Author's Note

Heyyyyyy...

Yeah—you. Before you clutch your pearls, let me warn you:

This book has a lot of sex in it. Because let's be real—I know what the girlies like.

But Body Count is more than bodies on a bedpost. This is about the stories behind the count. About why a woman might add one more notch to her lipstick-stained mirror. About how nobody ever tries to tally up the reasons that pushed her there. Just the bodies she collected along the way.

Because isn't it funny how a woman's body count is everybody's business. Men out here high-fiving their boys, forgetting half the names (and sometimes the condom), but we're the ones labeled reckless?

So yeah—this is for my girls. The ones who own their choices or are still learning how. The ones who've been bruised, used, amused—and somehow still soft enough to try again.

And while you're reading, Keep an open mind. Because everyone's experience with sex, love, heartbreak (and revenge) is different. Us women gotta stand up for each other—because these men have been standing up for each other's trash behavior since the dawn of time.

So, to all my ladies: I hope you laugh, side-eye, maybe even tear up a bit—and most of all, I hope you enjoy the ride. Rate and review when you're done so this story can keep finding more sisters who need it. I love y'all down.

And I hope you enjoy this book—straight from Netra's Notebook.

PS: Disclaimer—

Let's keep it a buck. I'm not saying some of y'all ain't out here hoeing for no reason, because babyyy... some of you absolutely are. This book is not for you. If you're out here breaking innocent hearts and collecting souls like Pokémon cards just because you bored? Go heal, sis. For real. Hit up www.therapyforblackgirls.com and let the good Lord and your therapist tag team that spirit.

Trigger Warnings

Before you dive headfirst into this messy masterpiece, let me give you the real:

This book has a lot of sex. Like, enough to make your church auntie clutch her pearls twice.

It features men being humbled, hearts being snatched, egos deflated, and more than a few "sis, please don't" moments.

It also tackles **grief, betrayal, mental health, loss, and how sometimes the heaviest heartbreak doesn't come from lovers—but from life itself.**

So, if your heart is tender or your spirit's already doing the absolute most, **pause and check in with yourself.** Protect your peace first. The story will wait for you.

Because at the end of the day?

Every orgasm, every drag, every tear-stained paragraph in here is all for a **good cause:**

A woman learning to love herself harder, to sit in her grief without letting it bury her, and to make the whole damn world kneel at her altar—just like she deserves.

Read responsibly. Hydrate. Take breaks. Text your therapist or your group chat if you need to.

And most importantly, **enjoy.**

Love,
Netra Antionette

Playlist

1. Getting Late – Floetry

2. Just To Be Close To You – The Commodores

3. Crazy About Me – KenTheMan

4. Freaky Freestyle – KenTheMan

5. Typa – GloRilla

6. Unloyal – Summer Walker & Ari Lennox

7. Ex For A Reason – Summer Walker, JT & City Girls

8. F.N.F. – Hitkidd & GloRilla

9. I Hate You – SZA

10. Over – Lucky Daye

Scan the QR code for more....

1
Rivah

I watched him suck the whipped cream off every toe—and I mean every toe. He did okay. His tongue wasn't as advanced as it should've been for someone with his big age, but I guess.

Everything was going fine until he tried to spray that shit on my vagina. That's when I knew—either he didn't get much pussy or he messed with women who didn't take care of themselves. Because how do you not know that it can give someone a yeast infection?

I almost left right then and there. But I had to see the process through—for the blog. I'd been hyping up the girls all week, and with all that mouth he had? Yeah, I had to see it through.

He tried to talk dirty.

"Yeah, you like that, huh? Told you I was gon' ruin you."

I blinked at the ceiling, unimpressed. "Mmhmm."

He was all ego, whispering things he clearly thought were filthy and seductive. But to me, it was giving podcast energy—like he spent more time listening to men talk about women than actually listening to women.

"Yo body made for me," he groaned, gripping my thighs.

"Wow. That's crazy," I said, reaching for a pillow.

When he finally leaned back and gave me room to switch positions, I smiled to myself. **Game time.**

I got on top and took over with no warnings. The kind of rhythm and depth that came from experience and knowing your own damn body. Within seconds, he was grabbing his sheets trying to hold on.

"Wait, wait—daamn!"

He was gasping, sweating, mumbling something about how he didn't know it could feel like that.

I kept going until his voice cracked, and he let out the kind of moan that sounded like it came from the bottom of his soul. Like he released some childhood trauma.

By the time I slid off of him, he looked like he needed IV fluids. He reached out lazily, trying to pull me closer.

"Damn, girl. Come lay down. Just for a minute."

I stood up, grabbing my dress.

"Aww, I'd love to, but I gotta get home. Long day tomorrow," I said, slipping my heels on like I didn't just give the man an out-of-body experience.

He sat up, dazed. "You gon' call me later?"

I paused at the door, puffing out my curls.

"Uhh... we'll see."

I stepped outside, letting the sun hit my skin while I slid my sunglasses on. The click of my heels echoed down the steps as I walked off—another man humbled, another entry for my blog.

As soon as I made it home, I went straight to the shower. I needed to rinse the day off me—working all morning was one thing, but more than anything, I needed to wash off the remnants of a man who did everything but please me in the ways he'd spent nearly two weeks hyping up over text.

Once I stepped out, I grabbed my towel from the warmer and dried off slowly, then slipped into my favorite fluffy white robe. I pulled my curls into a full, messy bun and did my quick skincare routine.

"Alexa, play Megan Thee Stallion," I said, already knowing I needed something to match my mood.

"Shuffling music by Megan Thee Stallion," she echoed back.

The beat dropped, and I knew the song immediately. I threw my hands up—face serum still on—and started twerking in the mirror as I rapped along:

"Ain't nobody freak like me,

Give ya what you need like me,

Ain't nobody got on they tip-tip-toes

and rode to the tip like me..."

I smirked at myself in the mirror. "Exactly," I said, still bouncing to the beat while rubbing in my moisturizer.

I headed into the kitchen and started my Keurig for some tea. While it brewed, I pulled out last night's honey-glazed salmon and tossed it in the microwave.

Most women with a two-bedroom apartment might turn the extra room into a glam space or a walk-in closet. Mine was my sanctuary. My creative escape. A room covered with wall-to-wall paintings of women's bodies—different shapes, sizes, shades. Curves, stretch marks, softness and strength. Quotes layered in gold script that screamed body positivity.

Every inch of the room reminded me: *She is hers, entirely.*

She is not yours to measure, judge, or shame. She moves how she wants, gives when she chooses, and owes no one an explanation.

"Alexa, cancel," I said, and the music fell into silence as I took a seat at my desk. I bowed my head and closed my eyes.

"God, thank you for getting me through another day. Thank you for this food I'm about to receive. I pray that it's a nourishment to my body. Amen."

NETRA ANTIONETTE

BODY COUNT: Entry #MindYoBiz

By Soaked

750,000 followers strong & still drippin'

Title: Mr. Turtleneck & the Case of the Positive Test

Ladies.

First of all, before I drag today's subject by his non-circumcised situation, I want to say thank you. We've officially hit **750k readers**. That's 750,000 women (and a few nosey men) who are choosing to take up space, own their stories, and talk about pleasure without shame. I'm honored to be your anonymous bestie in the shadows.

Let me say this loud and poetic for the ones in the back:

A woman's body is not a battleground for respectability.

It is a home. A temple. A playground. A kingdom.

And she decides what to do with it—how, when, and with who.

Men give their bodies away like expired coupons and get praised for it. But the moment we explore our own, they want to call us everything but free. So to that I say:

Touch who you want. Taste what you crave. And don't you ever feel bad about it.

Now... back to the star of the show.

Mr. Turtleneck.

I know, I know. Ever since I told y'all he sent me that unsolicited pic and I noticed he wasn't circumcised, the comments have been rolling in.

"Girl, it's better!"

"You ain't lived until you've had one!"

"Trust me, it hits different!"

Well, to all 342 of y'all who said that...

Step to the front of the class.

Because you all get a **fat F.**

Matterfact? A damn E.

That shit was TRASH—with a capital T.

Red Flags I Ignored (So Y'all Don't Have To):

1. **He claimed he was single.** Cute.

2. But if you're single, why—*WHY*—did I go to his bathroom, open that middle drawer under the sink (because I always do), and find a **positive pregnancy test?**

3. That was Red Flag #1.

4. **Tree Hut Watermelon Sugar Scrub in the shower.**

5. Now listen. I'm not saying men can't exfoliate. But I smelled him. I felt his skin. Ain't no damn way he's the one using that. That scrub wasn't for him—it was left behind. Or worse... currently shared.

6. **The way he tried to claim me after one round of mediocre motion.**

7. He had the audacity to say, *"Your body was made for me. Nobody else gon' do you like this."*

8. Sir. You just got a D-minus in foreplay and failed penetration 101.

Experience Rating: 3/10
+1 for effort.
+1 for ambiance (his sheets were clean).
+1 because the salmon I ate after I left was fire.
Would not recommend. Would not repeat.
Song of the Experience: "Unloyal" by Ari Lennox & Summer Walker
Because nothing about him was loyal—not to the truth, not to hygiene, and definitely not to the woman who left that pregnancy test in his drawer. Whew.
What's Next?
Will we have a new prospect?
Or will we spin the block on a fan favorite?
Drop your predictions in the comments.
Remember: I test these theories so y'all don't have to.

Body count? Nah. Character development.
Because a woman who chooses herself is never out of line—
She's just out of reach for the ones who couldn't handle her.
Stay wet, stay wild.
— **Soaked**

2

Rivah

"Alright class, folders out and brains on—today's science lesson is about the most complicated, overworked, and underappreciated thing you'll ever own…"

I turned dramatically toward the whiteboard, pen in hand like I was about to change lives.

"The human body."

A few of them ooohed like I just said something magical. One of my students, Teelamiyah, already had her hand up. I ignored her. She always had a hand up, even if I asked if anyone didn't have a question.

"Now, some folks will tell you the brain is the most important organ. And yeah, it does help you read and write. But let's keep it real, your body is out here doing hard labor, even while you sleep."

I grabbed my glittery purple marker and wrote across the board in large font: **BLOOD. BONES. BRAINS. BUTT.**

There was a collective gasp. A few giggles. Somebody whispered, "She said booty…"

"Yup. I said it. Because I keep it factual. And because your gluteus maximus—which is the real name—is the biggest muscle in your entire body. It helps you sit, stand, walk, run, and yes… dance."

"Miss R! You said a bad word!" one of the boys called out, his eyes wide like I just cussed in church.

I tilted my head. "Baby, I said a science word. Y'all gon' thank me when you're the only kid in third grade who knows the real name for your butt."

They laughed. They always do. And that's the thing about third graders—you teach them better when you say things like you mean it.

I pointed to the human body diagram I'd drawn: eyes big, teeth bigger, arrows pointing to every part I could label without getting a parent email.

"Now let's break this thing down. Bones? They're the scaffolding system of your body. Basically, you're built like Legos. If you didn't have bones, you'd just be a walking jellyfish."

"Ewww!" someone yelled.

"Exactly. Y'all would just be flopping around the classroom."

More laughter.

"And blood? Blood is like the Amazon Prime of your body—it delivers oxygen, nutrients, and even little white blood cells that fight off germs. Like when you ate Takis off your friend's desk and then started coughing three hours later."

"EWWW!!"

I held back a smirk. "Don't act like y'all don't be doing it."

I leaned against my desk and crossed my arms, feeling like the Beyoncé of bodily functions. I'd like to see someone else explain the lymphatic system with this much flavor.

Just as I was about to go on a rant about skin being the body's saran wrap, the bell rang.

And like clockwork, my teacher's assistant Miss Cierra popped up in the doorway with her clipboard and her pressed smile.

"Okay friends, line up for your daily activity!"

I gave her my best "they're all yours now" grin. "Come get your babies."

The kids scrambled to pack up. Backpacks zipped, chairs screeched, and Teelamiyah (hand still raised) whispered to me on her way out, "Miss R, I'm gonna tell my mama my booty helps me twerk."

I blinked. "Tell her Miss R said it's called your *gluteus maximus*... and it helps you *dance*."

As the last kid skipped out of the room, I finally exhaled and grabbed my cold cup of coffee. My brain was already switching gears.

Little did they know...

They had just learned about the body.

And I always wrote about one.

NETRA ANTIONETTE

I never wrote blogs at work. I'm not dumb. Ain't no way I'm logging into my little scandalous corner of the internet from a school computer. One click too many and next thing you know, I'm trending on Teacher TikTok for all the wrong reasons.

I could bring my personal laptop... but nah. Something about the school Wi-Fi gives "government surveillance" vibes. I don't trust it. I don't even let my personal phone connect to that demonic Wi-Fi.

So, I did what I always do during my free period. I pulled out my phone and opened the blog app. Comments were still rolling in fast days later.

Everyone wanted me to spin the block.

Like... bad.

They were in my comments heavy:

"Sis, don't make us wait weeks for some new man with no rhythm."

"You owe us a second chance date night. You the reason I started texting my toxic ex again."

I know I asked for feedback, but damn. They basically told me to pop it on a handstand like I ain't got groceries to buy and papers to grade.

But I'll admit... they weren't wrong. I was ovulating, hot as a hot pocket, and craving something with seasoning. That man from a few nights ago had left me high, dry, and emotionally itchy. A disappointment. Like sugarless Kool-Aid.

Then I saw a thread of comments talking about **"Titty Milk Tyrone"**.

"We need another round with the Mama's Boy."

"I know he's too close with his mother, but you rated a 6/10. That's practically husband material in your world."

"He's probably been waiting by the phone since the last time you pulled out the driveway."

Well... A 6 out of 10 is high for me. That's basically a Yelp four-star review with potential.

So... I opened the blog app and hit "New Entry."

BODY COUNT: Quickie Post

By Soaked

Title: Spin-the-Block Saturday Is Loading...

Y'all really bullied me into backtracking. But I hear you.

After a very disappointing encounter with *Mr. Turtleneck*, the votes are in and the streets have spoken. Loudly.

So yes.

Yes, I will be doing a *Spin-the-Block Saturday* with Titty Milk Tyrone—a.k.a. the only man to get a 6/10 from me and still get left on read.

We'll see if he's taken any of the notes I left him with. We'll see if he's graduated from the mama-made cartoon sheets to real grown man behavior. I'll let y'all know in a few days.

Homework better be done. Extra credit wouldn't hurt, either.

Stay tuned. And remember—

Body count? Nah. Character development.

xo,

Soaked

NETRA ANTIONETTE

My bestfriend Vane's house always smelled like coconut oil and ambition. The soft buzz of her nail drill hummed under Summer Walker playing low in the background, and I sat in her kitchen like I had a hundred times before, palms up and heart guarded.

"You only get these long French tip claws for one reason," Vane said, twisting her mouth up like the judgmental auntie she swore she'd never become.

I smirked. "Yeah, they are some cute little grabbers, but Mr. Spend-the-Block and anybody else thinkin' they up next? Not getting a damn thing."

Vane rolled her eyes and tapped the brush against the powder. "I can't wait until you find a man that makes a believer outta you. And have you doing all the things you swore you'd never do."

I laughed, but not all the way. "Yeah, we'll see."

She knew. Vane had been holding my secrets since we were fifteen. When I broke, she was the one scooping the pieces off the bathroom floor, wiping mascara off my chin, telling me I was still beautiful through hiccups and heartbreak. She knew why I walked heavy and loved light.

Growing up, it was always, *"Men like this; men want that,"*—aunties preaching like they had some secret to purity. "Men value women who don't give it up." "Be careful who you let touch you, baby, 'cause you gon' carry that forever." Judgment disguised as wisdom, and I ate it up.

I stayed with my first love from ninth grade until my freshman year of college. While everybody else was "giving it up," it was a known fact: Rivah Renée Banks wasn't giving up shit. I was the girl you bragged about. My boyfriend acted like it was an honor to have me on his arm, like my "no" made him some kind of king.

We even planned our first time like it was something sacred. I never said I was waiting for marriage, but he was gonna wait until I felt like he earned it. That was the deal.

Then I came back to campus a day early from visiting my parents. I walked into his dorm and found him with his face buried between the thighs of the same girl whose viral video had just been making rounds—her with four football players like she was trying out for the damn team. The same girl he used to talk so bad about.

But there he was—deep in it. Face first. Looking like he was bobbing for apples in that thing while she laid back with her eyes closed like she was on a spa retreat.

They didn't even hear me come in.

And when I saw that, my stomach turned. Literally. I walked straight over, stood above them and threw up on both of their naked, nasty asses. Didn't say a word. Just let it out—right on his back and all down her chest.

And you know what? I hate throw up. So once I saw my own, I did it again. Spun from side to side like a damn lawn sprinkler, making sure everybody got a taste. And then?

I calmly wiped my mouth, stepped over his socks, and walked right out the door.

After that, I did what everybody said was the best.. "heal."

You know—"Pour into yourself," "Focus on your goals," "Choose you."

So I did. For six straight months, I kept my head in my books, stayed out the way, and somehow ended up in the arms of a man who seemed perfect.

He was in his last year of undergrad before medical school, sharp as hell, well-spoken, and came from one of those families that made you feel like you stepped into a Hallmark movie when you visited. They lived not too far from campus, and we'd go over there just to chill. His mama would hug me longer than she hugged him. His daddy would ask me how school was going. I swear, they liked me more than they liked their own damn son. He was the lucky man I gifted my virginity to.

At the time, I thought he had set the bar high. Turns out the bar was in hell.

I finally gave him some. I thought it was good. I was thinking this was it, and I was finally safe.

But nope. Plot twist.

We'd been together over two years when he planned this big romantic-ass picnic in the campus garden. Candles, wine, a Bluetooth speaker playing our song—all that shit. I just knew that man was about to propose. The way he was crying, holding my hands, telling me how much he loved me and how he couldn't lose me.

Yeah. That's when he hit me with it:

He got somebody pregnant.

And not just anybody. *Cheyenne.*

Everybody in the state of Antionette knew that the girl's knees stayed bruised and her throat had no gag reflex. Trains weren't a rumor—they were a damn weekend activity for her. And this man—this educated, grown-ass man—got her pregnant.

But he wasn't done.

He said he still wanted to be with me. He said he didn't want to lose me but we'd have to be quiet about our love from now on. Lowkey. Said if Cheyenne even smelled that he was still with me, she'd take him and his whole family for everything they had and never let him see his baby.

Now I don't know if that girl even had that kind of power—but the fact that he believed it? That he let fear lead instead of fighting for what he claimed to love?

That shit was the ugliest thing I'd ever seen.

And I don't love dumb niggas, so that was the end of that.

I laughed right in his damn face.

Wiped my fake-ass tears and stood up like the goddess he couldn't keep.

"You know what's wild?" I said, brushing crumbs off my lap. "You got the degrees, the charm, the family, and the fake 'man of God' act. But underneath all that? You're still just a weak, pitiful little bitch with commitment issues and community dick."

He blinked like I slapped him.

Then he said, "Can I at least get one last kiss?"

I tilted my head, gave him the softest smile I could conjure. "Yeah... I guess."

He leaned in slow, eyes closed like we were in some sad-ass movie.

And just as his lips touched mine—

I opened my mouth and bit the hell out of him.

I bit his bottom lip like it owed me money.

Felt the skin break and the blood hit my tongue like copper-flavored karma.

He screamed, pulled back, hand to his face. "Rivah—what the hell?!"

I licked my lips slowly and stood tall.

"Let that be a warning for the next nigga that plays with me. He might not be so lucky."

And I walked away with blood on my lip gloss and peace in my step.

I wasn't gon' let him, or anybody, see me sweat.

But the second I got back to the dorm with Vane, I cracked like glass.

We were both walking and breathing depression at that point. Just two sad-ass besties, heartbroken and hollowed out, existing off Hot Cheetos, cheap wine, and trauma bonding.

Vane had just been dumped by her boyfriend of three years—her first, too.

He told her she was too much of a good girl.

What type of brain-dead bullshit is that?

At first, I thought, "Well... at least he was honest."

Until she said his fantasies included seeing a random cute girl at the mall, pulling her into the bathroom, and turning it into an impromptu orgy.

I paused.

Like... okay, everybody got their preferences. I'm not one to kink shame.

Then she added that he refused to wear condoms because it "ruined the experience."

He also wanted everybody to do oral as well like it was a damn human fondue party.

Now look, I ain't never been nobody's purity police. You grown? Do your thing.

But baby, health is wealth. We are not about to be out here swapping STDs like library books.

"You get a STD! You get a STD!" Hell naw, I ain't Oprah.

I might've done some things, but let it be known— I wasn't out here kissing *nobody* in the mouth, wasn't giving nobody no damn oral exams, and sure as hell wasn't raw-dogging my way through life.

Then one day, we were in our dorm, laying on opposite beds, wrapped in fuzzy blankets and sadness, listening to Mary J. Blige.

And somewhere between "Not Gon' Cry" and "I'm Going Down," I sat up and turned that shit off.

I said, "Enough."

That was the day my life changed.

I stripped off every expectation they ever tried to stuff down my throat about what a "good woman" should be.

The way they tried to braid shame into our hair and stitch guilt into our panties.

How they said your worth was in your ability to be untouched, unbothered, and unseen.

Nah. Because women deserve to be wild and worshiped. To explore their cravings without consequence. To stretch, scream, and savor every ounce of pleasure this life has to offer—whether it's for one night or none at all.

Because my body isn't a battleground for someone else's insecurities.

It's a damn altar—and I choose who gets to kneel.

I was done with love, yeah.

But I wasn't done with experience.

I love what skin feels like under fingertips.

I love the art of pleasing someone and the science of knowing how to please yourself.

And the day I stopped caring what people thought about how I moved, was the best damn day of my life.

Of course, my best friend Vane had comments. She's been in a relationship for three years, acting like she is holier than thou with a lil glitter on her Bible. But sis... when you are in a full-blown love story with a woman named Bubbles who switches between using a strap and her own vagina depending on the moon cycle, your judgment gotta come with a disclaimer and two forms of ID.

Everything she says goes in one ear and slides out the other like lube on a latex glove.

But I love her and that's my girl. I'm the only one who can say that kind of shit to her. She's the only one allowed to judge me to my face—because let somebody else try it, I promise you, I'll make the room get real silent.

My humor's like a funeral with punchlines.

When I'm finished, it'll be so dark, even God might look away—and I'll be the only one still laughing.

"Where are you headed after this?" Vane asked, giving my nails one last approving look. They were perfect. Long, sharp, French tips with just enough attitude to start an argument and slap somebody's mama.

"Dinner with Titty Milk Tyrone," I said, laughing while scrolling through my phone. That man had been blowing me up. I left him on read for weeks, but the moment I finally texted him back, he started double texting like we were working on a damn group project.

"I hope it goes well for you. I'll catch the update later."

Only she knew I was the voice behind the *Body Count* blog. I couldn't let that part of me ever bleed into my career—not with the work I did and the kids I loved. Rivah Banks was a respectable, licensed, soft-spoken professional by day... but at night? I was the anonymous chaos that kept half the city clutching their pearls and locking their phones.

As I stood up, I grabbed my purse and looked at her with a smirk.

"You pray for me, okay? 'Cause if his head game is still trash, I'm giving him your number just to piss you off."

Vane threw a nail brush at me. "Bitch, bye!"

We both laughed and hugged, tight and long like always.

And just like that, I was on my way to dinner reading his text.

> I miss your taste and I ain't talkin' 'bout your cooking.

God help us all.

3

Rivah

The restaurant was nice. Like, linen napkins and water-poured-from-glass-bottles kind of nice. Five stars. Mood lighting. A jazz trio in the corner playing something that made you wanna undress slowly. I had to give him his credit. Titty Milk Tyrone understood setting the damn tone.

He looked good, too, dressed in a tailored navy suit that hugged all the right places. His beard was freshly lined, and he smelled like cocoa butter confidence.

The conversation was actually good. He talked about his job as a project manager, how it was stressful but fulfilling, how he liked building things from the ground up. I nodded, engaged, even asked a couple follow-ups just to be polite. It was giving responsible. It was giving stable.

But baby, I didn't get these claws sharpened and my legs smooth for no damn TED Talk.

At some point, I gave him that look. The "I appreciate your passion for working like a man should, but the day ain't getting no longer and neither is my patience" look.

He smirked like he already knew what time it was.

Still, I had to give him three points for the meal. I'm a firm believer that expensive food is foreplay. Feed me something I can't pronounce and keep the wine flowing.

He grabbed the check without hesitation and just slid his black card like a man who wanted to be remembered. I smiled, classy and cute, and let him take my hand as we left the restaurant.

Because let's be honest—if a man pays top dollar for my filet mignon and two glasses of imported Pinot Noir, I can at least hold his hand to the car.

We stood by valet, the air breezy. He turned to me smoothly and said, "You can leave your car here. I'll bring you back later after we swing by my place."

Now see...

That was cute. But also? Hell no.

Because if I need to get the hell on down, I don't have time to be waiting around for no Uber. I keep my keys within arm's reach like a black mama keeps a belt.

I smiled sweetly and said, "Mmm, no thank you. I'll follow you."

He didn't argue. Just nodded and walked to his car.

I followed behind him in mine, playlist queued and lip gloss reapplied, ready for whatever was next.

We pulled up to his house, and I had to admit, it was nice. Clean landscaping, fresh paint, even one of those fancy doorbells. The kind of place you wouldn't mind being seen walking out of in yesterday's clothes.

But listen, there's a reason I called him *Titty Milk Tyrone*.

I parked in the driveway, and like a gentleman, he opened my car door and helped me out. We walked in, hand-in-hand, and as soon as the door closed behind us, I caught a whiff of food.

Not his food. It smelled like smothered something and greens that had been cooking all day and I knew damn well that man couldn't cook like that. I gave him a quick side-eye.

"My mom wanted to come spend some time with me," he said casually. "So, she's in the guest room. You know she had to cook a meal."

I smiled sweetly and nodded like I gave a damn, but the second he looked away, I rolled my eyes so hard they almost touched heaven. I'm not saying your mama can't come visit, but why is it every single time I pull up, she just so happens to be here too? You couldn't text her, *"Hey Ma, not tonight. I'm tryna score"*?

But that wasn't my business. And I wasn't there to argue about his mama.

I took my time walking through the house. I'd never gotten the full tour, and it showed. Everything was styled too well—cohesive, minimal, thoughtful.

He grabbed my hand and led me down the hall to the master bedroom. R&B was already playing low, and the lighting was moody as hell. Okay, points.

He turned to me and smiled, then dropped to his knees to take off my heels and started rubbing my feet.

"I missed you," he said, hands working magic. "These last few weeks, you have been on my mind heavy."

I leaned against the wall with a small smirk. "I can't talk to you every day. I can't let you know how much I really like you. If I do, you'll stop chasing me."

That was a lie. I barely liked him at all, but I knew how to play the game. Stroke his ego just enough to make sure he performed at maximum effort. And with the way my hormones were behaving, I needed every ounce of it.

He kissed my ankle first, then moved slow—up my calves, thighs, stomach, chest—tracing each curve like it owed him something. When he finally got between my legs, he took his damn time and for once, I didn't flinch.

And baby, he was doing his thing.

Like, the man had taken notes. Every bit of constructive criticism I'd ever given? He must've been studying it like flashcards.

Then he turned me over.

All fours. My favorite.

I was just about to start thanking God when he leaned down and put his whole damn face between my cheeks.

"Oh... okay!"

He earned another three points for that. That brought him up to a seven, and he still hadn't even inserted himself yet.

It was shaping up to be an amazing night.

Until—

"Can you be a little quieter?" he whispered. "I don't want my mom to hear."

...What?

I blinked. Almost all my moisture vanished. My coochie almost dried up like the Sahara.

I laughed. But he should've known better—because that wasn't a real laugh. That was the laugh before I ruin a man's ego on purpose.

So when he finally inserted himself, I screamed. To the top of my lungs.

Not from pleasure, but from pure disrespect.

Because why are you too damn young to say "no" to your mama, but grown enough to invite a woman over here and ask her to be quiet while you hitting it?

I started throwing it back hard and with intention.

Enough to shake the bedframe and make him lose rhythm. He was in a trance, fighting for balance, and didn't even realize how loud I was getting.

And that was exactly the point. I wanted his mama to hear every single damn thing.

I climaxed first. He followed shortly after, barely able to hold himself up.

Then—

KNOCK. KNOCK. KNOCK.

"Oh shit," he mumbled, scrambling to grab something to put on. He handed me my clothes like we were mid-heist.

I blinked. Confused. "What?"

"She can come in," I said, slowly slipping on my panties. "We got the same damn thing."

He looked pissed, but didn't argue.

His mama stormed in, arms crossed, lips twisted. "I can't get any sleep in this house with all that nasty business going on! I'm trying to rest while you are here with your woman friend doing all that damn hollering."

That pissed me clean off. He went to calm her down. I started putting my clothes on for real, cause baby... the vibe was done.

He had dropped back down to a three. Just like that.

They were still going back and forth in the hallway when I walked out. I went straight to the kitchen, stood there with my keys in hand, and cleared my throat loud as hell so they'd shut the fuck up.

"Thank you," I said, smoothing my dress.

"Dinner was nice. And the after was mid because the knocking was cringy as hell. Y'all have a good night."

I turned and started heading for the door when I heard his mamma.

"She ain't got no home training. Just a skank."

I stopped, wheeling around slowly.

He looked at me with big eyes like he already knew I was about to go TF off.

"Skank?"

I calmly met her eyes, keys still in hand, smiling like I was about to offer her a piece of pie.

"I'm very smart, ma'am. And if I'm not mistaken, skank means a sleazy or disreputable person and that's not me. So clearly, you must be talking to one of your personalities, because it damn sure ain't me."

Her mouth dropped open, but I wasn't done. Not even close.

"I came here as a guest. A classy one. I tried to be polite while your grown-ass son was asking me to moan in whispers like this was an episode of National Geographic."

She blinked, stunned, and I took a step closer—just enough for my voice to stay low, calm, and cut her straight to the bone.

"Now, I get it. It's hard out here for single women of a certain age. Real hard. I imagine it must be lonely laying in that guest room night after night, listening to your son knock somebody else's walls down while yours have been in foreclosure since the '90s."

Tyrone whispered "Rivah..." behind me, but I held up one finger like—stay in a child's place.

"And another thing," I continued, folding my arms and tilting my head like a mother about to read a report card. "You ever wonder why every time a woman shows interest in your son, you magically need to 'come spend time with him'? Like clockwork. Every. Single. Time."

I smiled again, sweet as molasses.

"It's almost like you think you're his woman. Which is weird, because last I checked, you carried him—not dated him."

She gasped, clutching her pearls.

"So here's my advice—from one woman to a lonely one..

Get yourself a man. Or a hobby. Hell, a rose toy. Anything that'll keep you from playing eavesdropping gatekeeper at your son's dick appointments."

I took a step back, adjusted my purse on my shoulder.

"And next time you want to call somebody a skank?

Make sure your son isn't the one handing out his meat to her."

I blew her a kiss, turned to Titty Milk Tyrone, and winked.

"You were almost somebody in my life."

I turned toward the door, ready to make my dramatic exit and let the night fade into the "never again" section of my memory.

But no, his mama started talking again. Like she didn't hear me the first time.

So out of respect, or curiosity, I turned right back around.

Hands on hips. Eyes narrowed. Respectful, of course. Because that's just the kind of woman I am.

She cleared her throat and turned to her son first.

"I'm done lying for you," she said, with a tight voice full of pride and passive aggression. "I will not be disrespected in my own house."

Titty Milk Tyrone looked like he wanted to say something, maybe even tell her to shut up—until she shot him a look that made his whole spine straighten. He went silent real fast. That titty milk must've turned into whole milk the way he shut down.

She smoothed her blouse and kept going, chin lifted.

"My son is a hardworking man. He's been through a lot. He didn't have the credit to get this house on his own after some... financial problems, so I put it in my name for him. That's what mothers do."

I raised an eyebrow but let her cook.

"He's working as a custodian right now at a job site, but he's hoping to work his way up to project manager. And I have a history in banking, so I help him manage his money to make sure the bills are paid on time. Without my guidance, he wouldn't have been able to maintain all of this."

She motioned around like we were in a luxury estate.

"I'm a mother who wants the best for her son. So yes, I come to spend weeks here—because I can, and because I like being around him as much as I can."

She finished her little monologue with a proud nod, like she just cleared up world hunger.

I clapped.

"Aww," I said with a sweet smile. "I just wanna say... you're a good mom. For real. It's beautiful how much you want the best for your son."

She softened just a little, smug like she thought I was about to back down.

"But... your son is thirty-seven," I added, sweet as peach pie. "And way too old to be lying about his damn life."

Her smile dropped.

"There's nothing wrong with falling on hard times. We've all been there. I've needed help before. Ain't no shame in that. What is shameful is your 37-year-old son lying through his veneers, talking about he's a project manager with equity in this house, when you are out here covering every financial wound he has with your old bank statements."

I pulled my phone out of my purse and scrolled with intent.

"You should see the way he texts me," I said, waving the screen. "Bragging about all the things he owns, all the places he built, all the money he moves. And not once—not once—has he mentioned you. Not your sacrifice. Not your name. Just him. So maybe instead of defending him, it's time to reevaluate all this 'guidance' you keep giving to an ungrateful grown-ass man."

She looked like I slapped her with a warm biscuit.

Then I turned to Titty Milk Tyrone.

"And you? You had the nerve to ask me to whisper during sex in a house that's really your mamma's?"

Sir.

You are not a man, you are a dependent with stamina."

He opened his mouth to speak but I put up a finger. "Shhh. Save it for your group chat."

I gave them both a tight smile, pulled my bag up onto my shoulder, and headed for the door.

"Y'all enjoy each other's company tonight. I won't be back."

And his point total reset to zero.

NETRA ANTIONETTE

BODY COUNT:

BLOG ENTRY #MindTheBizThatPaysU

"Spend the Block Saturday: Never Again."

I will never listen to y'all again.

No, for real. I mean that from the depths of my spirit. Because y'all hyped me up, talkin' 'bout "Give him another chance, sis!" and "Maybe he matured!" and "Sometimes a good meal is the beginning of healing!"

Well guess what?

I've been traumatized.

So don't look for me next Saturday. Don't ask me to reflect, forgive, or revisit anything that's not buried and blessed in the group chat. Because my block is back on do not disturb permanently.

Now... let's get into it.

First of all, we may need to change his name. He is no longer *Titty Milk Tyrone*.

From here on out, he is **Whitney Houston**.

Why? Because babyyyyy—he has **Nothing. Nothing. NOTHINNNGGG** and not even ME.

And I mean that from the bottom of my cash app.

Okay, now he did set the tone with dinner. Five-star vibes. Beautiful ambiance. Food had me blushing.

He even rubbed my feet like he just finished watching a 90s love story.

And then things went left because his mama wanted to co-star in my show. Y'all.

Please... PLEASE start paying attention to a man's relationship with his mama.

Because these mama's boys are out here doing the absolute most.

They are not just close with their mamas, they're emotionally married.

Like, I'm convinced some of these women think they gave birth to their husbands.

This man had his mama in the next room while he was trying to flip me like a pancake and then had the nerve to ask me to "keep it down."

Sir?

You're grown enough to beg for booty but not grown enough to tell your mama to go stay at her *own* house?

The experience was cute—for the first 17 minutes.

But after the post-nut argument and the "guest room" showdown, I left with more regrets than I did calories burned.

So let's get to the official *Body Count Rating*:

Rating: 0/10.

Would not recommend. Would not revisit. Would not even share a meme of this man.

I wouldn't even wish this date on my worst ex's new girl.

And listen—men be out here talkin' 'bout,

"Women need to have their own,"

"Bring peace,"

"Be soft,"

"Be a feminine goddess with a six-figure career and no previous baggage,"

Meanwhile THEY out here needing their mama to cosign the damn mortgage.

How your mama got better credit than you and a stronger WiFi signal in a house you claim is yours?

Bottom line: If your man's mama can walk into the room in the middle of a stroke and call you nasty?

You're not dating a man.

You're dating someone's dependent.

Song of the Night?

Let's go with "How I Look" by GloRilla because that's exactly how I felt walking out that man's house while his mama stood there looking like she wanted to file a noise complaint.

How I look letting a man stroke me in silence while his mama stirs greens in the next room?

Also—again, I repeat:

We're officially retiring *Titty Milk Tyrone*.

From this day forward, he shall only be referred to as:

Whitney Houston a.k.a. **Peter Pan** because clearly, he never wants to grow up.

Anyway, that's all I got for today.

I'm about to go soak in a hot bath, pray to the ancestors, and delete all text threads with anyone born before 1996 and still using their mama's Netflix password.

Until next time—

Love, chaos, and condoms,

—Soaked

4
Rivah

My kids were taking their science test, and I was doing everything in my power not to lay my whole face on my desk and flatline.

I had already blinked too long twice—long enough to scare myself.

I was holding on for dear life until my free period. Just a good 45 minutes of peace where I could close my eyes, fake like I was answering emails, and maybe drool a little if the Lord allowed.

I looked up at my class—all little heads down, pencils scratching, papers shuffling. I cleared my throat and stood up.

"Alright y'all, you've got five minutes left. Wrap it up. If you're still working after that, you'll have to stay behind while the rest of the class goes to activity."

They started working faster, like I had just threatened to cancel Christmas. I took a deep breath and sat back down, digging in my desk drawer for my emergency stash.

There it was. My enemy, but best friend.

I had promised myself I was laying off of energy drinks. But that's what I get for staying up late binge-watching *Insecure* for the sixth time. It wasn't even a new season, so it wasn't mandatory. But *Insecure* is one of those shows you have to watch at least once a year—just to remind yourself that nobody has it all figured out, and that's okay.

Even if your life looks like a hot mess sometimes. Even if you've got a secret blog, a situationship or three, and a classroom full of tiny humans counting bones and asking what a "gluteus maximus" is.

I took a sip, leaned back in my chair, and whispered to myself like Issa in that mirror:

"You got this, girl. Just don't fall asleep with your mouth open."

The bell rang and *thank God*. I didn't yell it, but I felt it in my soul.

One by one, the kids turned in their tests and walked out the door. Peace was within reach, but of course, it's never that simple. Because here came **Teelamiyah**. It's always Teelamiyah. Never misses a moment to say something that makes me question the birth rate.

"Miss R," she said, clutching her Lisa Frank folder like she had breaking news, "My dad's coming to the school fundraiser tonight. I showed him a picture of you from the old yearbook and he said you're pretty."

I smiled politely. "Aw, how sweet," I said, tilting my head. "But baby, if he's anything like you, I wouldn't give him the time of day."

She blinked at me, confused.

"You talk too much and ask too many questions. And if that's genetic? I'm good."

Her mouth dropped open just a little, and I had to bite the inside of my cheek to keep from laughing.

I cleared my throat. "Tell your daddy I appreciate the compliment, though. I'd love to meet him—but I'm way too fabulous to be anybody's classroom stepmom. That's not in my ministry. Having you for eight hours a day is already my limit. I'm good."

She nodded slowly, like her little brain was trying to decide if I was serious. (I was.)

As soon as the last kid shuffled out, I turned the lock and let out the breath I'd been holding all morning. I slid into my desk chair, ready to take that sweet, sweet nap. I had just closed my eyes when it hit me.

School Fundraiser. Tonight.

My eyes flew open and I whipped around to look at the wall calendar.

Fundraiser Night.
Assigned item: SWEETS.

I sat up so fast I knocked my energy drink clean off the desk.

"I didn't bake shit," I whispered, grabbing a sticky note like that was gonna help me manifest 100 cookies outta thin air. I slapped it on the desk, stared at it, then let my head fall forward in full chaos mode.

And then I remembered: **Vane.**

I pulled out my phone and called her. No answer, and that pissed me off.

I checked her location and she was at home, so I called again.

She picked up, sounding slightly out of breath. "Hello?"

"Ew. Bitch, what are you doing?"

"Being grown."

"Oh yeah? What's your anatomy of choice today?" I asked, smirking.

We both fell out laughing.

"I actually called with a favor."

"Oh Lord," she groaned. "You calling me with sweetness in your voice? You need something."

"I do. I need 100 cookies. Baked. By 4PM."

There was a pause. A very judgmental pause.

"I'll Instacart the ingredients to your door. All you gotta do is channel your inner Nara Smith and work that oven like your rent depends on it."

She blew into the phone so hard. "You better be glad I love you... and that I'm a little bored."

"You the best, for real," I said.

Then her tone shifted. "You good, though? Like, really good?"

"I'm fine. Why are you asking like somebody died?"

Silence.

"Hello?" I said.

Vane exhaled again, but this time it wasn't playful.

"So... you don't know?"

"Bitch, no! What the fuck are you talking about? You're acting like somebody—"

"Rivah," she said slowly.

"Girl, if you don't tell me, I swear I will stick these long-ass nails down your throat and scratch everything down there."

She hesitated one more second.

"Conner's dead."

My heart didn't break. It just... dropped.

"Oh. Damn."

I wasn't sad, exactly. More like... shocked. That was someone who'd been a chapter. A long, dramatic, plot-twisting chapter.

Conner was the one I gave my virginity to. He was smart but slow and had community dick. But still, he had mattered, once.

"You hadn't talked to him in a while, huh?" Vane asked.

"Nah. It's been a year. Real short convo, too. He tried to hit me with the 'Cheyenne's kid ain't his after 10 years' of playing daddy mess. I hung up so fast, my phone screen cracked."

Vane laughed softly. "He had that sandy-ass red hair too."

"Right?! And still thought that baby was his. Said it ran in his family. His great-grandma or whatever had red hair. I hate a dumb nigga," I said, cracking up.

"That's crazy... You just talked about him on your blog."

"I know. Life really be lifin'. One day, you're writing about bad head and blocked numbers. Next day, you find out the dude who fumbled your flower is pushing daisies."

"Are you sure you're okay, though?" Vane asked again, gentle now.

I paused. Then said with a sigh, "Girl, yeah. I'm okay. I mean... I'm a little shook. Not from grief, but like... damn. Another ex off the Earth."

Vane snorted.

I leaned back in my chair. "But for real—I'm okay. Life is short, and Conner was a wild ass memory. That's all. Now go make those damn cookies. Bake 'em like we're trying to win him back from the grave."

She cackled. "You are so sick."

"And yet... delightful," I said sweetly. "Let me know when my snickerdoodles rise."

We hung up, and I sat there for a second. Staring at nothing. Not sad. Not happy. Just reminded.

I pulled out my phone and scrolled through the archives until I found the post I wrote about him about three months ago.

BODY COUNT:
Entry #WasteOfAPoppedCherry
By Soaked
Title: DNAin't Yours
Whew. The girls been asking about him for a while.
"What about your first?"
Let's take a lil stroll down memory lane, shall we?
Though, honestly... This is one of those memories that deserves to stay distant. Like "don't even wave if you see me in public" distant.
I really liked him. No, scratch that—I borderline loved him.
He was tall, smelled like generational wealth, and had that calm energy that makes you want to sit on his lap and talk about childhood trauma. He checked every box—good convo, good credit, grown-man career, and a good stroke for his age.
But unfortunately...
He forgot to keep his damn rocket in his pocket.
I'll never forget the day he told me that he was "gone be a daddy."
Now listen—I believe in second chances. I believe in growth.
But I do NOT believe in making a life with a man who made one with a woman that wore ankle monitors with wedge heels.
And the kicker? He didn't even get a blood test.
He was so deep in delulu land, he said, *"I can just feel it. That's my baby."*
Sir, you couldn't even feel that she was lying to you.
But go off, Daddy Daycare.

He swore up and down it was his, even though the math was mathing all wrong and the baby looked like the neighborhood ice man. You know—the one with the lazy eye and the jerry curl.

And still… he stayed. Like a good little Captain Claim-a-Kid.

Fast forward to now. The child is damn near middle school age and guess what?

DNA says: You are NOT the father.

It's giving: **99.9% Dumb.**

It's giving: **Maury should've been involved in the group chat.**

It's giving: **The D was great but not worth the lifetime of headache or the STD paranoia.**

Because if y'all knew what his BM been here doing…

Whew. I just know that D has a lil bit of fire and brimstone going in and coming out. But hey—not my business.

I wish him well, I really do. I hope he finds healing, therapy, and a girl who actually ovulated when he thought she did.

But one thing he won't find? **Me.**

Not when he realizes the grass ain't greener and tries to run back over here talking about how "I was always the one."

No baby. If the grass ain't green over there, spit on it 'til it grows. Use all your damn saliva until it's a forest, bitch.

Song of the Post: 'Baby Mama' by Fantasia

Because this whole situation felt like a BET movie with bad lighting and wigs.

Ladies, sometimes, the D is good.

Sometimes, the vibes are right.

Sometimes, the future looks real damn fine from the passenger side of his truck.

But, choose you.

Even when he smells like potential.

Even when your legs want to betray you.

Even when he calls you late at night talking about "just come talk."

You're not the one who needs to prove her worth—he's the one who needs to realize it before he loses access.

Because we don't do reruns around here.

Body Count? Nah. Character development.

xo,

Soaked

NETRA ANTIONETTE

The gym smelled like cupcakes, folding chairs, and overcompensating parents. I stood behind my little cookie display.

I didn't bake a damn thing, but my presentation was flawless. I just knew they were about to sell like Beyoncé tickets. I had them stacked neatly on a table draped in glittery tulle I found in the back of the PTA closet. And I even printed a little sign that said:

"Support Science & Sugar." Look at me—marketing queen.

Before I could fake like I was adjusting something, the assistant principal Mr. Dale came strolling over with his clipboard and networking smile.

"Miss R!" he said, like I wasn't already regretting this evening. "There's someone I'd like you to meet—this is Mr. Hamilton, one of our school's top donors."

Mr. Hamilton looked like he owned a country club, a boat, and at least three retirement accounts. He stuck his hand out with a smooth smile. I shook it, giving him my best professional fake charm.

"Mr. Hamilton was just asking about our science scores," Dale added. "Your students are scoring the highest in the district."

"Well, you know," I said with a wink. "I make science make sense."

They laughed way too hard at that. Mr. Hamilton wiped a tear from his eye like I was comedy royalty. "You're such a fine young woman," he said. "Are you single? My son's a high school teacher. Teaches algebra."

I smiled, sweet but uninterested. "Oh, that's kind, but I'm taken."

I lied. Because listen, if he teaches, too, what are we gonna do? Sit around after work and grade papers together?

Talk about our students over frozen lasagna? Compare who got cursed out worse that day? Oh hell naw. I work hard enough; I don't want to come home and hear about his kids cussing, too. I was mid-rant in my head when I felt a tap on my side. I already knew who it was.

Teelamiyah. Of course.

As much as I didn't want to be bothered by her and her daily questions about bones and bugs and if God was a girl—I was lowkey grateful she interrupted that awkward matchmaking moment.

"Miss R," she said, "my daddy wants to meet you."

I turned around, adjusting my smile until I saw who was grinning at me from across the gym like he just won a raffle.

Oh, hell no. I busted out laughing. "Baldy Locs!"

I reached out to shake his hand out of habit, pure chaos on my face.

I didn't call him Baldy Locs just to be mean. I called him Baldy Locs because he swore up and down that his hair was "longer than most women's," meanwhile his locs were fighting for their lives, holding on by hope and a prayer. He had full-on thinning with soon-to-be bald spots right in the middle of his scalp.

Teelamiyah looked confused. "His name is Marcus."

"Mmm. Yes. Mr. Marcus," I said with a tight smile. "You have such a lovely daughter. She's very... vocal. Smart. Never stops talking. I see the apple didn't fall far from the tree."

His smile dropped quicker than my expectations.

He turned to his daughter. "Baby, can I have a minute with your teacher?"

"Sure!" she said, skipping off like her presence wasn't just the plot twist of the night.

As soon as she was gone, he looked at me. "Why haven't you returned any of my calls? Or texts?"

I folded my arms, stepping back just enough to let the energy get awkward.

"First of all, you lied. About having a kid. That's Red Flag #1, Marcus."

He opened his mouth like he had an excuse, but I kept going.

"She's a little annoying sometimes—asks 500 questions before lunch. But what kid isn't? She gets on my last nerve, but guess what? I love her more than you do apparently, because ain't no man on this Earth about to have me out here lying about a whole human I created."

He looked around like he wanted the floor to open up and swallow him. No such luck, boo.

"And if we really wanna keep it real, you wanna know the real reason I ghosted you?"

He blinked. Hard.

"The stroke. Sir. It was bad. Like, no rhythm bad. Like, 'Is this a warm-up or are we done?' bad. The way you lied with confidence, I just knew you were gonna back it up. Instead, you gave me three minutes and a motivational speech about why it was my fault you nutted fast."

He looked like his soul left the building.

"You out here lying about having a child, lying about your hairline, and lying on your meat? Be serious. You were mid-thrust, talking about how no one ever made you feel this way. Boy, you were barely making me feel anything at all."

I took a bite of one of the fundraiser cookies and chewed dramatically.

"So yeah. I ghosted you. Because the only thing worse than a bad stroke is a bad stroke attached to a liar. And baby, you're both."

He didn't say a word. Just stood there, ego deflated, probably wishing he'd sent his child to a different damn school.

"You know what's wild? Now I gotta sit across from your daughter every morning and pretend I didn't sit on FaceTime seeing you butt-naked last spring."

He blinked.

"Good talk," I said, still chewing. "Enjoy the fundraiser."

I tried to walk off with just enough attitude in my hips so every piece of fat in my ass jiggled. I wanted him to see what he fumbled, what he lied to, and what he would never circle the block for again. Because the audacity of a man with thinning locs and secret kids trying to circle back was truly beyond me.

I was genuinely proud of myself for ghosting him when I did. The man was out here moving like a childless king when he had a whole daughter—and probably a few extras. That's what I be saying. **Men lie, and society shrugs.** But let a woman lie about having a child? She's a monster. A sorry-ass mama. A walking Lifetime movie with a missing moral compass.

I was still mentally dragging him when I caught a glimpse of Teelamiyah heading in my direction, eyes locked like a missile with a question locked and loaded. I dipped off immediately, slipping into a quiet little corner near the punch table.

That's when I heard him.

"You look like you're hiding out."

I glanced sideways and saw him—chocolate, tall, relaxed confidence in the way he leaned against the wall.

"Maybe I am. Maybe I'm not." I gave a polite smile and a subtle eye roll, mostly out of habit.

He smirked. "You know you got that unapproachable energy, right?"

I turned fully toward him, raising a brow. "Oh, do I? Hello then. I'm Rivah. So nice to meet you, Mister…?"

"Kross, with a K."

He said it low, smooth, like it rhymed with trouble.

"Nice to meet you too, Rivah. It's very nice," he added with a slow smile that somehow made my stomach flip. And not in a professional way.

I heard someone shout, *"Miss R!"* in the distance. Sounded like one of my students or somebody's overly invested mama. Either way—I turned back to Kross real quick and struck my best "deep in conversation" pose.

"So, Mr. Kross. What brings you to a school fundraiser? I'm sure there's a club, lounge, or at least a strip club calling your name."

He laughed—deep, sexy. "I'm actually here as a donor. Been one for a few years now."

I blinked. "Oh? Donor? Okay, you fancy."

I eyed him. "What's your line of work—if you don't mind me asking?"

"I'm an engineer."

I turned my face up. "An engineer? You don't look smart enough—" I paused with a grin. "No offense. But I've never seen an engineer look like this."

And I meant that.

Chocolate skin, Muscles that told stories under that button-down. A clean, trimmed beard with just enough curl at the edge. And don't get me started on his smile.

He wasn't iced out or screaming money, but the watch, the subtle cufflinks, and the perfectly tailored slacks whispered wealth. Not the flashy kind. The "I'm set for life, and so is my mama" kind.

"Looks can be deceiving, Miss R," he said. "I saw you setting up your little cookie table. I wouldn't have guessed you were an elementary teacher, either."

I raised a brow. "Oh yeah? What do I look like I do? A lot of people say nursing or law."

"Honestly?" he said, rubbing his chin with that damn smirk again. "I was gonna say... OnlyFans."

I sucked my teeth.

"Especially with all that ass you tooting around. How the hell them nine-year-olds supposed to focus?"

I rolled my eyes so hard they did a backflip, but I laughed anyway.

"Shut the fuck up," I said, trying not to smile too much. But he saw it. He knew it.

And I hated that I liked it.

I was just about to say something slick about his beard when Kross hit me with a look that said he already knew what I was thinking. That man was dangerous. The kind of dangerous that doesn't come with warnings—just clean cologne, good credit, and dick discipline. Or so I hoped.

Before I could say anything else, I felt someone walk upon me.

"Rivah, can I talk to you for a second?"

I didn't even have to turn around to know it was Baldy Locs.

I glanced over my shoulder, then back at Kross and raised my eyebrows. "Don't you see me talking to my nigga?"

Kross didn't even flinch. He just smiled slowly and looked at Baldy Locs with that classy-psychotic calm that could end someone's life and still get invited to dinner.

"I'm sorry," Kross said smoothly. "I hate to interrupt your reunion tour, but it looks like she's already on a better program now."

Marcus looked like someone just stole his dignity. "My bad," he muttered and shuffled off like he was trying not to cry.

I stood there blinking, shocked. Not because of what Kross said—but because most men just laugh and play along. Smile awkwardly. Maybe hold my purse like a good little placeholder.

But him?

He threw shade with precision. Said it with his chest.

And I liked it. A little too much.

"Damn," I said, finally exhaling. "That was impressive. What you just did for me? I know that's gon' cost me."

He tilted his head. "I'm glad you know, and I'm not cheap either. I charge top dollar."

"Damn. I didn't know you were really out here letting hoes buy you."

He smirked. "Only you."

That made my stomach drop and my thighs clench, and I hated it there.

I squinted up at him. "What do you want from me, anyway? Do I look like the type to let you hit on the first night?"

"I mean..." he said, pretending to consider. "I've never really understood why women make such a big deal out of that."

"Uh, because we tryna avoid getting ghosted? Ain't nobody tryna have a man moaning in her ear one day and blocking her number the next."

Kross chuckled, hands in his pockets, relaxed. "Rivah, I can ghost you after the first night or I can wait three months, meet your mama, fix your cabinet door... and still ghost you. Either way, it's a fifty-fifty shot."

I stared at him, lips parted.

"...You're not even wrong," I muttered, laughing in spite of myself.

There was something about him. Something I couldn't name yet. But I felt it in my stomach and my chest—and a little bit lower. He knew it, too. He kept licking his damn lips like he knew exactly what they were doing to me.

Maybe it was his honesty. Maybe it was the way he looked at me like he'd already undressed me in his head and still wanted to know my favorite color.

Maybe I was still ovulating. Who knows.

But I leaned in and said, "Maybe after this fundraiser... we could go get some tea."

He smiled, lazy and lethal. "Tea it is."

"I'll meet you in the front lobby at 9PM."

"Bet. I'll be the one smelling like bad decisions."

5

Kross

The front lobby of the gym was nearly empty with just a few stragglers saying their goodbyes, adjusting folding chairs, and scooping up leftover cupcakes nobody had room for. The fundraiser had been a success—donations were flowing and the PTA would be doing cartwheels by the next meeting.

I had shaken the necessary hands. Flashed the expected smile. Mingled with donors and district colleagues. But through all of that, I never once took my eyes off her.

Rivah.

The name suited her—flowing, fluid, soft at first glance but powerful if you dared step in too deep.

She was posted near the back of the gym, talking to someone with that half-annoyed, half-amused look she wore so well. Her curly hair was still cascading down her back, catching the light in the way only natural curls could. That bounce. That volume. She was sunlight and storm wrapped in one body.

Her outfit was professional enough to give off an elementary school teacher, but fitted enough to tell the truth about that body she clearly couldn't apologize for having.

Business skirt, modest blouse, and heels. And every time she moved, I noticed something new.

The slight arch of her foot. The way her gold bracelet tapped against her wrist when she talked with her hands. The smirk that showed up when she was about to say something smart or unhinged—or both.

Most people wouldn't notice that. But I noticed everything.

She had a little spice to her. That edge under the soft. That bite behind the smile.

Some people would call it snobbish. I call it necessary.

In a world full of pick-me's and passive energy, Rivah moved like she chose herself every time—and anyone who couldn't keep up got left where they stood.

I liked that. Scratch that—I loved that.

I loved that she could handle herself in any room. I'd watched her laugh with donors, cut a grown man down with a single sentence, and charm a crowd of nosy parents like she wasn't actively plotting her exit the whole time.

She was the kind of woman I could take to meet my mama or take to the hood fish fry and she wouldn't flinch at either. She'd know when to keep it polished and when to cuss somebody out over a game of spades. My kind of woman.

I'd finally been close enough to smell her perfume and hear her laugh in real time.

And, there was no way I was walking away.

We agreed to meet at 9, and if she was the woman I thought she was, she'd either show up early… or exactly two minutes late just to prove a point.

Yeah. She was gonna be a problem.

But I liked problems. Especially ones with full hips, rolled eyes, and no filter.

She rounded the corner at 8:59 on the dot, walking like she had a secret and smiling like she knew she was about to ruin someone's peace.

"Right on time," I said.

She raised an eyebrow. "Please. I'm only here for the tea and because you did me a favor. That's it."

I smiled, slow and unbothered. "Good. I'm only here for the company."

She looked down at her phone, smirking.

"Well, would you look at that," she said. "It's 9 o'clock. And all the cafés and tea spots I like in town… just so happen to close at 9."

She hit me with that sarcastic, fake-disappointed smile.

I laughed, shaking my head. "You're slick."

"I'm honest," she shrugged, like her intentions weren't dressed in lipstick and a test I was supposed to fail.

I didn't flinch. "You got tea at your place?"

She blinked, slowly, with that "nigga please" energy.

"I do," she said. "But only men who don't have a place of their own ask about going to a woman's house."

I let her have that—for half a second.

"I got a place," I said casually. "In The Toast."

Her eyes got big before she caught herself and tried to act regular again, adjusting her stance like that didn't impress the hell out of her.

The Toast was it. The top gated community in Stonehaven, Antionette. Where the old money lived, and the new money got vetted twice.

"Well," she said, chin up, voice smug, "good for you. I'm glad you have a home."

"But," she added, her tone dropping into that slick sass, "I don't know you. So you're not coming to my house. And if you really want some tea, I guess we can go to The Toast. *If* you even really live there."

I laughed harder this time, leaning back against the wall like her little games weren't working—when really, I was loving every second.

"I don't have shit to prove to you," I said smoothly. "And just like you don't know me—I don't know you. You might have sticky fingers... or worse."

She raised an eyebrow, clearly not expecting that.

"I'd hate to do you something real bad," I added, voice low, calm. "So, if I'm not invited to your home... Neither are you to mine."

The way she looked at me?

Shocked, but turned on.

Like she couldn't believe I had the balls to say it... and loved that I did.

"I like you."

Her voice dropped—playful, but honest.

"You're not thirsty. That's not something I'm used to."

I shrugged. "There's too many women in the world for me to be thirsty over one who hasn't even given me a reason to be.....yet."

She licked her lips and tried to cover up her smile, but I caught it. I always catch it.

"There's a hotel about a mile away," she said, turning slowly. "Fancy place. They have some really good tea."

I grinned. "The Bella Nucia?"

"Yep," she said, already walking off like the main character. "Ain't nothing cheap about me. Even conversation costs top dollar."

And I followed her—no rush, no pressure.

Because I knew one thing for sure:

I could afford it.

NETRA ANTIONETTE

The lounge inside Bella Nucia was dressed like luxury had something to prove—dim lighting, soft jazz, velvet chairs, and servers that knew when to bring your drink and when to leave you the hell alone.

She sat across from me in a dark wine-colored booth, legs crossed like she was trying not to accidentally destroy me. Her lip gloss had a sinful sheen under the chandelier light, and her voice was low and smooth.

"Let's be clear about something," she said, sipping her tea like it wasn't laced with danger. "Whatever happens tonight doesn't go beyond tonight."

I leaned back, watching her without blinking.

She kept going.

"And if it does? It'll be on my terms. My call. So there's no need for you to know anything outside of my name."

I smirked. "Noted."

"You already know where I work," she added, tapping her nail against the cup. "And for a man like you, that's already too much. Knowing anything else?"

She met my eyes, bold and unbothered.

"Would be signing your own death certificate."

I laughed. Not shaken, but definitely turned on.

Because it wasn't a threat. It was a warning. And warnings only matter when you plan to come back.

I leaned forward, voice low. "That's cute. But if dying means tasting you first?"

I tilted my head and smiled.

"Then go ahead and engrave my name on the damn stone."

She paused. Her eyes twitched the way they do when you're trying not to admit that you're turned on. She sipped her tea again like it would cool her off.

I could see the heat rising in her chest. Could feel her legs shifting under the table. She wanted me just as bad as I wanted her—but she still had to win. Or at least pretend like she was still the one holding the leash.

She tilted her head now, voice syrup-sweet.

"Maybe..." she said, tracing her finger around the rim of her cup, "we should stop playing and get a room."

I didn't flinch. Didn't blink.

I just reached into my blazer pocket, pulled out the key card, and slid it across the table.

Room 614. Already waiting.

"I'm ten steps ahead of you," I said calmly. "And that's crazy for a woman who thinks she's in total control."

Her expression didn't break. But her eyes lit up.

She took the key, stood up slowly like she wanted me to watch, and I did. She leaned in over the table. Then, without a word, her hand trailed down... and landed square on the print in my pants.

She rubbed—slow, confident—and leaned in close to whisper right in my ear: "Oh, you'll find out real soon who's in control, Kross. And spoiler alert?"

She gripped a little firmer and smiled.

"It's always gonna be me."

And just like that, she turned and walked toward the elevators—hips talking louder than her mouth ever could.

I sat there for a second, catching my breath like I'd just been hunted.

Because I knew something she didn't:

She could think she was in control all night. But I never play a game I don't plan on winning.

Rivah's heels hit the floor, soft but commanding. She tossed her purse on the velvet chaise, unbuttoned the top of her blouse, and turned to me like we were already mid-scene in some private film only she could direct.

Her eyes said one thing, but I had other plans.

I shut the door behind me and leaned against it, watching her undo the second button. Slowly. Deliberately. She moved toward me with heat in her walk and purpose in her mouth.

"You're just gonna stand there like you're afraid of me?" she teased, already halfway out of her clothes.

"Nah," I said calmly. "I'm not afraid. Just focused."

"On what?" she asked, biting her lip, unbothered. "The fact that you're about to have the best night of your life?"

I smirked. "Tempting. But no."

She raised an eyebrow.

"I want to know what I'm getting myself into."

That made her pause. Slightly.

"I'm serious," I said, crossing the room and sitting down in the armchair, legs wide, arms resting on my thighs. "Soul ties are real. I need to know what kind of spirits I'm about to get attached to."

She laughed. Actually laughed. "Nigga, what?"

"I'm deadass," I said. "I want to know about your childhood trauma and shit."

She tilted her head like I was joking. But then she realized—I wasn't.

"You're serious?" she asked.

"Very."

She sat on the edge of the bed and looked at me for a second. Her smile dropped into something more real. Still guarded. Still dangerous. But softer now.

"Well," she exhaled. "I don't have daddy issues, if that's what you're fishing for."

Her voice didn't crack, but I felt the shift. Her eyes darted to the side before locking back on me.

"My dad raised me. And he was damn good at it, too. Up until he died when I was eighteen."

My chest tensed. But I didn't move.

"My mom?" she said, shrugging. "She passed giving birth to me."

Then she smirked. Dark. Beautiful.

"I guess I've been too much from the beginning. Even my mama doesn't have the energy to deal with me."

She said it like a joke, like it didn't hurt. But I saw the flicker in her eyes. The flash of something raw she hadn't meant to give me.

She looked away like she regretted saying it.

That's when I got up.

I crossed the space between us slowly, knelt in front of her like she wasn't on display, and brought my hand to her cheek. She blinked at me, still wearing that sarcasm like armor.

I leaned in and kissed her.

Not like a man who wanted to fuck.

Like a man who wanted to learn the shape of her sadness.

I kissed her like I was making love to her mouth alone. No rush. No hands tugging. Just mouths moving slow, lips searching, breath syncing.

She inhaled against me, and when she exhaled, I swear it sounded like relief.

I didn't say anything when I pulled back. I didn't have to.

Her lips were still wet from the kiss. Her body was still, like she was trying to figure out what the hell just happened between us.

But she recovered fast. Started to reach for my shirt like she was reclaiming the night and reclaiming the power.

She thought she had me right where she wanted me, and I wanted her to think that. Because the most dangerous thing you can give a woman like her is the illusion of control.

I didn't need to prove her wrong. Not yet.

I wasn't there to dominate. Not right then.

I was there to learn her. To experience her without rushing.

To let her believe she was leading—while I mapped every inch of her soul.

I undressed her slowly, like I was unwrapping something sacred. Kissed down the slope of her shoulder, along her clavicle, the curve beneath her breast, the dip of her stomach. She tasted like something I wasn't supposed to want but couldn't stop reaching for.

And when she was bare, standing in nothing, I pushed her back onto the bed. Just enough to watch her legs fall open like instinct.

She didn't even hesitate.

She wanted me just as bad as I wanted her.

I slid out of my pants slowly, still holding her gaze. Her eyes dropped and—

Yeah. They got wide.

She blinked like she wasn't expecting what she saw.

Like the rumors she never heard were suddenly all true.

The length. The width. The weight of it.

All front and center.

I reached into my pocket, pulled out the condom I'd brought—because planning was power, too—and rolled it on while looking her dead in the eyes.

I stepped between her legs and grabbed myself, smacking her pussy lightly, a few times—watching it bounce, pink and swollen and begging for attention. She was so damn pretty between the thighs. Full. Warm. Inviting.

And I gave it to her.

No words. No noise. Just a slow, deep entry.

She gasped and her nails dug into my back like she was bracing for something more than pleasure.

I moved slow at first, just enough to fill her and stay present in her eyes. I wasn't fucking for show. I was reading her—every blink, every moan she tried to swallow, every breath she held.

Her eyes watered, but not from pain. Not from fear.

From whatever the hell was burning beneath her hard-ass exterior.

She blinked it away fast, but I saw it. And I gave her an out—flipping her onto me, letting her slide on top.

Letting her take the reins and letting her lead.

She rode me like she was reclaiming territory, like she needed to leave her name on every stroke. She gripped my chest, rolled her hips in figure-eights, bit her lip like she was punishing me for all the men before me who fucked her body without trying to understand it.

And I let her think she was winning.

The sex was beyond good. It wasn't just physical—it was spiritual.

A collision of two people who swore they'd never need each other, but couldn't stop sinking into something deeper than they were ready for.

When she released, she clenched around me like she hated how good it felt.

And I held her hips while I followed.

She climbed off me like nothing had just happened. Like we hadn't just traded pieces of our soul without signing the paperwork.

She started getting dressed—cool, efficient, detached.

I stayed quiet. Until she slipped on her heels.

"Don't leave," I said.

She turned around, eyes hooded, lips glossy. "You didn't give me a reason to stay."

She did the final button on her blouse and looked at me like I was just another stop on a long-ass train she never planned to ride twice.

"You did what you came to do," she added. "So did I."

"You're doing what you want," I said, sitting up, voice calm again. "And I'm asking you—nicely—don't leave."

She laughed. "Okay, Kross. But newsflash—niggas never scared me."

She walked to the door, throwing a middle finger over her shoulder like a mic drop.

"I scare niggas," she said, loud and proud, right before slamming the door behind her.

And I laughed.

Because she had no idea—none—what she had just awakened.

She thought she was walking out with the power.

6

Rivah

I stepped out of the shower and grabbed my towel, wrapping it around myself before walking to the mirror above my sink. My mirror full of sticky notes.

Little squares of chaos and clarity. Quotes, affirmations, love notes to myself.

I stared at them for a second and opened the drawer beside the sink and pulled out my favorite black marker and a blank sticky note.

I wrote:

"Self care is moaning and a back arch in one."

I smiled, peeled it off, and added it to the glass—right between *"Your body is not a battlefield"* and *"Pleasure is a protest."*

Then I walked into my closet and slipped on my silk black robe because that's what the vibe was. Feminine, full, unbothered.

Still riding the high of everything Kross and I did… and didn't say.

He didn't just touch me. He studied me.

Let me think I was in control while he played chess with my whole nervous system.

I shook my head and smirked as I walked to the fridge. Normally, I'd make tea—my nightcap ritual. Chamomile and clarity.

But I needed water. That man had drained every drop of fluid from my body. Sweat. Spit. Sanity.

I cracked open the bottle like it was my last hope and chugged it halfway down.

Then I walked barefoot into my sanctuary. I sat in my velvet chair and pulled my silk robe tighter around me before waking up my laptop.

It was time to document.

To decompress.

To turn power into prose.

I cracked my knuckles, exhaled, and clicked "New Blog Post."

Because *Soaked* had something to say.

BODY COUNT:

Entry #CountYaOwnPockets

By Soaked

Title: He Met His Match... and Lost.

Okay, girls. This one's gonna stay between us, so don't go runnin' your mouths in the group chat.

Let me tell you about the time I thought I met my match.

He had the beard, the voice, the frame, the confidence... The resume was giving "I could handle a woman like you." And I believed him.

Now don't get me wrong... he was fine. Like, *"take my drawers off with a goodnight text"* fine. And the way he kissed me? Please. My ancestors felt that shit. I saw visions and I remembered all my passwords.

But when it came down to the main event?

Let's just say... he could handle it—

But, just barely.

Don't let these men lie to you. The pussy is the power grid, and baby, he hit a full-body blackout somewhere around position two.

It's no shade, though. The experience? **9/10.**

Why not a 10, you ask?

Because I rode him so good I had him seeing colors that don't even exist yet. And in that moment, I knew his mama made a hoe.

A hoe who got humbled.

Would I repeat? Absolutely.

Would I make him a regular? If I was *thirsty*... maybe.

But I'm not. So if he wants another taste, he better come correct and HUNGRY.

Closed mouths don't get fed, and this kitchen doesn't stay open past midnight.

To the girls:

Sometimes, the goal ain't to keep him.

Sometimes, it's just to rock his entire world, then dip before he remembers where he parked.

We are the prize. Not the package deal.

Eve didn't need Adam.

He needed her.

God looked at that man being bored, lonely, and unwashed... and said,

"Let me help this fool out."

That wasn't a favor to Eve.

It was a favor to him.

Moral of the story: **We don't need these men. They need us.**

Don't forget that.

And if you did?

Wake. TF. Up.

xo,

Soaked

NETRA ANTIONETTE

I crossed my legs and smiled, proud as hell at what I just submitted. I leaned back and closed my eyes for just a second—just enough to enjoy the peace.

Ding-dong.

I opened one eye.

The fuck...

I wasn't expecting any damn company. I got up slow, walked toward the kitchen, and pulled open the drawer where I kept one of many little friends stashed around the house. A Glock with a pink trigger. Just a little something pretty to match the vibe.

I padded barefoot to the fridge and tapped my security cam.

The moment I saw his face?

I laughed. Sarcastically. The kind of laugh that had a little disbelief, a little "I know you lying," and a whole lot of "boy, what?"

Kross.

Standing at my damn door like I'd ordered him on DoorDash.

I opened the door with my smile fake and my gun tucked behind it.

"What the fuck do you want, and why are you at my house like this ain't a scene in a damn crime show?"

He looked me up and down, cool and slow, with that same smirk he wore when I was bouncing on him like I was getting paid.

"I told you not to leave."

"I'm grown as hell," I said. "You don't tell me shit."

He stepped a little closer. "Oh, I know you grown. You rode me on your damn tip toes like you had a ballet scholarship riding on it."

My coochie smiled.

He leaned in, voice low and lethal. "I told you not to leave... because I was just getting started."

I blinked. Heat rising.

"I didn't wanna come to your house, but I don't leave jobs undone," he said. "You think you ran something. I let you have that. Let you build your ego, boost your little pussy power campaign. But, by the time I'm done? You won't be talking all that 'run the world' shit. That pussy gon' be dead and filing for disability."

...I almost drooled.

"I don't even know you like that to let you in my home," I whispered, breath hitching.

"You got a gun in your hand," he said casually. "I got one on my back."

He reached, pulled it from his waistband, and held it out handle first.

"Keep it close if you feel like you need it."

That was all it took. I opened the door wider and let him walk in. I followed behind him slow, gun still in hand, until we hit the living room.

He stopped near the couch. I placed both guns on the table next to the candles and incense like we were about to meditate instead of sin.

I faced the window, city lights twinkling through the glass. "Make a believer outta me."

And just like that, his hands were on my waist. His lips trailing fire down my spine. He took off my robe like he was unwrapping a curse he couldn't wait to be haunted by.

But, this time was different.

He didn't let me take control.

He moved me like I was his. Kissed me soft. Held me firm. He didn't fuck me—he humbled me. With every stroke, every whisper against my ear, he told me without saying a word: **you ain't the only one who knows how to run shit.**

I came once.

Then again.

Then a third time.

And by the time I was trembling beneath him, barely holding it together—I refused to tap out.

I had a reputation to maintain.

He was on top, staring down into me like he could see every dark secret I never told anyone. I said something filthy—something I knew would make a lesser man lose it.

He didn't even blink. He went harder.

I was supposed to win. But dammit... I kinda liked losing.

When he finally nutted, it wasn't loud. It wasn't dramatic. It was controlled. Like even that was on his own terms.

He stood up, dick swinging like a weapon. I was naked, still catching my breath, laid across the couch like melted gold.

He walked to the bathroom without saying a word.

I heard the water run.

When he came back out, he grabbed my robe and lifted me gently like I was weightless. Slipped it on. Tied it himself. Then kissed my forehead like we'd been together ten years.

I just sat there. Arms crossed. Watching him dress.

No words. Nothing to say. What the fuck do you say after that?

He grabbed his gun, walked to the door, then paused before opening it. He turned back to me with that same calm smirk.

"When I come back, just open the door."

Then he left.

I didn't know if I wanted to lock the door...

or open it wider next time.

BODY COUNT:

Entry #HumbledNotHeldBack

By Soaked

Title: Weak in the Knees (but I still stand on business)

I know.

I know.

"Damn Soaked, you back already?"

And listen... I know that's not like me. I usually take a few days to marinate, detox, and let the coochie and the spirit align before reporting back. But I'm not one to lie to y'all. I was humbled.

Yes, me.

Turns out, *homeboy was only warming up.*

What I thought was a full-course meal... was just the appetizer.

I'm lowkey scared to see what happens when this man hits championship mode. The stroke was consistent, the pressure was applied, and somewhere between rounds two and three, I think I saw Jesus tapping his mic asking if I was good.

Spoiler: I wasn't.

Now, I'm not gonna go into detail, because some of y'all read this at work and in church (*y'all ain't slick*), but let's just say...

I got pinned to a cross.

I ain't saying that man died for my sins... but baby, I might've confessed a few.

And no, don't get it twisted. I still run the world. Period.

But every now and then, it's okay to relax and let somebody else do the hard work. Sis was on PTO and he clocked all the overtime with no complaint.

Now, y'all know I love a nickname.

He left me somewhere between baptized and reborn...

Let's just call him **Holy Pressure.** Because *amen.*

Screenshot this moment.

Bookmark it.

Tape it on ya titty.

Because this is officially my first **11/10. Ever.**

And will it happen again? Highly unlikely.

So yeah... that's all for now.

Let's see if **Holy Pressure** wants a sequel.

Because I'm not thirsty...

But I am curious.

Body Count? Nah. This is Character Development.

"A woman's power ain't just in her body—
It's in knowing when to let it lead,
and when to let it rest."

7
Kross

Sunflowers.

I remembered her saying they were her favorite. I could still hear her voice like a taunt: *"Let the chase begin."*

So I chased.

Twice.

Had them delivered to her school. A big ass gold-wrapped bouquet each time, tucked with my number and one simple line:

> **"Still thinking about you. —K."**

And still... not a single response.

Not a "thanks," not a petty emoji.

Nothing.

I didn't chase women. That wasn't my lane. I studied patterns, managed teams, and moved in silence.

But she had me checking my phone like a damn groupie.

Seven days. That's how long it took for my pride to start whispering maybe she wasn't that into it.

But my gut said otherwise.

NETRA ANTIONETTE

Her name was Amira.

Brown skin, big curls, loud laugh. Checked every box on paper.

Dinner was smooth. She looked good, smelled better. Leaned in during conversation, giggled like she wanted more than wine. She reached across the table, her fingers brushing mine.

But every time she laughed, I heard *Rivah's voice* instead. Sarcastic. Sharp. Sexy as hell.

Amira said, "You should come back to my place," with that slow voice women use when they're already unzipping your pants in their head.

I nodded and went through the motions.

I sat on her couch, drink in hand, her legs in my lap, and all I could think about was how much I didn't care.

Her touch was too soft. Her perfume too sweet. She moaned when I kissed her neck and it annoyed me. Rivah didn't just moan. She gripped me by the throat and kissed like she wanted to win.

I stood up.

"Everything okay?" Amira asked, blinking like I broke character.

"Nah. I thought I could get my mind off something. Turns out I can't."

And I left.

I sat in the car for five minutes before I even got out.

I told myself I was just checking in. Just dropping by. Just proving a point. No warning. No text. No fucks given.

Three knocks.

She didn't open the door right away. But I heard movement.

When it cracked open, she didn't even let me see her fully—just peeked one eye out, her lips glossed, and her mouth already locked and loaded.

"You lost, or you just confused about what not using your number means?"

I smiled. "I sent you flowers."

"Yeah. Twice. And you still ain't get the hint?"

"That's the thing—I don't do hints. I do clarity. So, here I am."

I leaned on the doorframe, cool as ever, even though my jaw clenched the second I saw her in that robe again.

Black silk. Loose. Tied just tight enough to piss me off.

"Clarity? You pulled up to my house for clarity? Baby, this ain't a TED Talk. And since you like sending flowers, maybe next time send a clue too."

"I like when you talk shit. It gets me hard."

I saw her blink, and then that smart mouth curled into a smirk.

"You're probably hard now, huh?"

I glanced down. "Check for yourself."

She rolled her eyes, but I caught how her thighs shifted behind the door.

"So what—you thought just showing up was gone do something for me?"

"Nah. I just figured if you're gonna keep ignoring me, you could at least say it to my face."

"I don't owe you shit, Kross."

"Nope. You don't. But that doesn't mean I won't take it."

That made her laugh. One of those deep, belly laughs she tried to hide behind a scoff.

"You talk real confident for somebody who couldn't even get a text or a call."

"And you talk real distant for somebody who moaned my name like a prayer."

She went quiet.

"That's all you came here for? To be bold and delusional?"

I tilted my head. "I came here to see if that smart mouth still tastes like sin and contradiction."

"Mm. Depends. Are you still carrying that ego in your pants or have you finally learned how to use it?"

That made me laugh that time.

God, she was exhausting and electrifying all in the same breath.

I stepped a little closer. Close enough for her to smell me.

Her lips parted just slightly.

"You letting me in or what?" I asked.

"Why should I?" she whispered.

"Because I don't chase women, Rivah. But I came for you. And I don't come twice unless I plan on staying."

She sucked her teeth and swung the door open just enough for me to step in.

"Take off your shoes. And don't touch anything."

I stepped inside, shutting the door behind me.

"I'll touch only what wants to be touched."

She led me to her couch like she'd done it a hundred times before, but I knew better.

There was something different in the way her hips moved.

Rivah dropped her silk robe and stood in front of me with all that pretty confidence, lips slick with attitude.

"If you're as good with your tongue as you are with your dick, let me see."

I cocked my head, licking my bottom lip. "My tongue is sacred. I don't use it on just anyone."

She scoffed like that was the corniest shit she ever heard, but her legs were already shifting apart.

"I mean it," I said, standing up, stepping toward her until our bodies were a breath apart.

"I don't hand that shit out like it's a party favor. So if I do it... know that you're already special."

Her mouth parted, ready to run, but I wasn't done.

"And when I do eat you... when I eat your soul away... just know, when it's over—I'm fucking your face."

She burst out laughing, loud and wild like I told a damn joke.

"Yeah, right. A dick hasn't touched my throat since undergrad with my first."

That made me laugh, too. But not out of disbelief.

"Good," I said, voice low as I wrapped my hands around her waist. "That means it's rested. So when I eat this pussy, you're gonna return the favor... with gratitude."

She opened her mouth like she had a comeback lined up, something smart and slick, but nothing came out.

Her mouth was a problem. The kind of problem I'd pay to have.

She didn't just suck my dick—she owned it.

Like it was a damn art form. No gag reflex. No fear. Just spit and eye contact.

She took every inch like her throat had been preparing for this moment since birth.

And when she pulled off with that thin string of saliva still clinging to the tip? Goddamn.

If I wasn't holding onto the couch cushion, I would've folded right then.

And just when I thought she was done—when she thought she had taken everything from me...

I flipped her legs open and buried my face back between them.

Her body jerked like I shocked her.

She tried to grab my head and pull me up, but I wasn't done.

Not until she gave me that third one. That real one. The one that made her forget her name.

She came again, legs trembling, chest heaving like I stole the air from her lungs, so I let her rest.

She stood up, legs still a little wobbly, and walked naked to her kitchen.

"You want some water?" she asked, grabbing a bottle from the fridge.

"Yeah," I said, still catching my damn breath. "Might need electrolytes, too."

She laughed and handed me a bottle before sitting across from me in nothing but her confidence.

Then her eyes locked on mine and everything shifted.

"So... what's your full name?"

I raised a brow. "So, after I've been all up in your guts... You wanna know my name now?"

She shrugged. "Just seems fair."

I took a sip before answering. "Krossli Givelle."

"Krossli?" she echoed, lips curling.

"Yeah. Blame my mama. She wanted something strong but different."

She nodded slowly. Then her fingers drummed against the bottle in her hand.

"You know where I work. You've been to my house. You know what I look like under every light and angle. And yet... I didn't even know your full name and you don't know mine."

"You told me Rivah," I said with a smirk. "Was I supposed to ask for a government ID before I licked your spine?"

She smirked, but her eyes held that hesitation again.

"It's Rivah Renée Banks."

I let it settle. I rolled it around in my mind like a new favorite song.

"Rivah Renée Banks," I repeated. "That's beautiful. Got a ring to it."

"Yeah, well... I didn't say you could use it."

I laughed. "Then I'll earn it."

The air shifted again—still intimate, but weightier.

There were so many things I wanted to ask.

But I also knew better.

This wasn't the kind of woman you interrogated.

You just waited for her to unravel.

On her own terms.

And something told me she would.

8
Rivah

The acrylic dust was flying, scented candles were lit, and Vane was halfway through filling in my nails when she squinted at me.

"Okay," she said, flicking her eyes up. "Either you've been on a new diet or you're getting your back blown into alignment. 'Cause you look lighter."

I rolled my eyes, smirking. "Girl, maybe it's the prune juice I had yesterday. Cleaned me all the way out. I'm talking about shitting all day."

Vane laughed. "Nahhh. You glowing like somebody put 'holy pressure' on you. The blog post said that thang was good enough to rebaptize you."

I tried to hold it in, but the smile cracked through anyway. "Don't give me flashbacks."

"Mmmhmm," she sang, dusting off my hand. "Who is it?"

I bit the inside of my cheek. I didn't want to say anything because as soon as I did, the crazy in me would get activated. Detective mode. Page 38 of his Facebook photos mode. Find his old prom date and track her career path, too.

"It's just... nice right now. One month with a whole bunch of sweaty, borderline illegal sex sessions and a few decent convos. I haven't even looked through his socials yet because I'm tryna not be delulu."

Vane stopped filing and blinked at me. "Girl, don't blame that shit on me. You wanna snoop so bad but you tryna make it seem like I made you do it. This is how toxic starts."

I cracked up because it was the truth. "Alright, alright. His name is Krossli."

"Krossli?" she repeated, head tilted like the name jogged a memory.

"Krossli Givelle," I said. "He's an engineer. And when I say fine af, I mean distract-my-prayers fine."

Vane sat back like she just put two and two together.

"Wait... Kross?"

The air shifted. My heart dropped. "Please don't say it like that. Please don't tell me you know him, know him and now I gotta go back to mediocre D."

Vane burst out laughing. "Hell nah! Relax. That's Bubbles' cousin."

I blinked. "Come again?"

"Yeah! His dad and her mom are siblings. I've met him a few times at family stuff. Real chill. He got like three brothers and they all fine as fuck. Like it runs in the DNA or something."

I sat there in shock, blinking like a damn idiot.

"Small-ass world," I muttered.

But Vane was already grinning like we had wedding invites to send out.

"This lowkey makes me happy, though. You know he's never brought a woman around in all the years I've been around. Like ever. You might be the chosen one, ho. You know how cute it'd be to be in the same family?"

I looked at her. "Girl... chill. You are spiraling. Ain't no family. I don't even know what his mom looks like. We just got to the tea and forehead kisses part."

Vane smirked. "And?"

"And that's it."

Vane tapped the last bit of acrylic dust off my thumb and looked up. "Go wash your hands so I can seal you up and send you on your way."

I rolled my eyes but did what she said, sliding off the stool and heading toward the sink in her hallway bathroom. I was humming Beyoncé under my breath when I heard her yell.

"BIIIIIITCHHHHH!"

I whipped my head around like somebody just hit a scratch-off for $10,000. "Bitch *what*?!"

I was halfway back in the room when she turned her phone around, mouth hanging open.

"Look."

Big, bold headline:

Man Found Unalived in Home—Strangled.

Okay, that was weird. But what really stopped me in my tracks was the face on the screen.

My whole face twisted. "Wait—hold on. Is that...?"

Vane nodded slowly. "That's Bracelet."

I blinked hard. "Bitch."

Yeah... his name wasn't really Bracelet. That's just what I named him. Dude had an ankle monitor the size of a damn radio strapped to his leg like it was part of his wardrobe. I met him at a club—don't judge me—the lights were dim, the crowd was thick, and his beard was connecting. I ain't see the hardware until later.

"We only made it to date three," I said, plopping back down, stunned. "That was all I needed to know he was crazy."

Vane raised her eyebrows. "That's the one who told you not to wear crop tops, right?"

"Girl, he told me not to breathe sexy in public. Like... huh? Talking about, 'if I'm at home, why are you out?' Sir, because you can't leave the house! You're on house arrest! That bracelet wasn't just for decoration!"

We both laughed but I couldn't shake the chills that ran down my arms.

Vane's voice lowered. "That's crazy, though. First Conner, now Bracelet?"

I swallowed. "Yeah... that is kinda weird. I mean, Conner's death was a heart attack. At least, that's what they said. But Bracelet? That shit's personal. That was... up close. Hands-on."

Vane nodded. "He was in the streets though, right?"

"Yeah," I murmured. "Could've been anybody. He had enemies, for sure."

But still... two men I used to mess with, dead within weeks of each other?

I tried to shake the feeling crawling up my spine as Vane finished sealing my nails. "Yeah, you're right. Just weird coincidences."

But, the thought lingered.

NETRA ANTIONETTE

I had just stepped out of the shower, skin still warm and soft, when my phone buzzed on the counter.

Kross: What are you doing?

I smiled before I even picked it up. After our last sex session—where he folded me like laundry, I finally agreed to start texting him back. Not often. Not double-texting. But back. That was a big deal for me. I didn't like giving men access to me so easily. But he made it hard to pretend I wasn't curious.

Wouldn't you wanna know?

He didn't waste a second.

I do. That's why I'm coming to get you. Get dressed.

I rolled my eyes, even though I was smiling.

What if I say I'm not going?

Then I'll see you in 15 minutes.

I stared at the screen like he had me clocked. And damn if he didn't.

I slipped into my favorite chocolate dress—the one that hugged my body like it was scared to let go. Skin-tight, no room for imagination. If he was showing up, I was showing out.

Exactly fifteen minutes later—Ding. Dong.

Knock. Knock. Knock.

The doorbell and the three taps. Always the same. Always his signature.

I opened the door and there he stood in gray sweats like he wanted to start a fight. The print was printing. The way his eyes roamed my body like he was already undressing me made my thighs press together on instinct.

He tilted his head, that smug smile creeping across his lips. "You wearin' that? You really don't want us to make it where we're going, huh?"

I raised a brow. "Oh, I thought you were in charge tonight?"

He let out a short laugh and nodded. "If I step in that house, we're not making it five feet. Grab your purse and come on."

I smirked, turning around slow enough to let him watch the switch in my hips. Grabbed my purse from the counter, then tossed my hair back over my shoulder on the way to the door.

He didn't move. Just stood there like a statue built for sin.

"Let's go," I said, brushing past him.

I wasn't gonna lie... when I opened that door and saw gray sweatpants with a print that had its own heartbeat, I almost forgot I was supposed to be playing hard to get.

Almost.

He looked me up and down like he was proud of what he saw. My dress was tight, but that's the point. I don't dress for men, but if they happen to choke on the sight, that's their problem.

The car ride was smooth. He drove like he had good credit and somewhere important to be. The small talk we made was light, flirty, with just enough bite to keep me on my toes. He pulled up to a little café I'd never seen before and said, "Give me just a second."

I watched him walk off, those sweatpants swaying like they knew they had power.

When he came back, he had a tray full of drinks and a small brown bag. Didn't say a word. Just smiled and handed me a cup.

We didn't stay there. Instead, he drove again, this time to a downtown parking lot where you could see everything but still be ducked off in the corner like you had something to hide. I liked that. I liked that a lot.

He turned the car off and started unpacking the bag like it was a damn picnic.

"Here's your tea," he said, handing me the cup. I took it and smirked. "Okay, come through with the tea and ambiance."

Then he opened this container full of what looked like strawberry aliens.

"What the hell is that?"

He laughed, like I was a child asking about taxes. "Dubai chocolate strawberries. Edible rose petals, pistachio, gold flakes... it's real sexy."

I squinted at it. "So you brought me flower food?"

"Just try it," he said, holding one up like he was feeding grapes to a queen.

I took a bite—and baby, my soul clutched its imaginary pearls. I tried to keep my face neutral, but I knew I failed. That shit was criminal.

"Okay," I muttered, still chewing. "That's illegal."

"Told you."

I sipped my tea and glanced at him. He wasn't looking at the crowd outside like I was. He was looking at me.

"So, what's this about?" I asked, raising a brow. "It's late."

He shrugged. "I love parked conversations. And when I thought about who I wanted to talk to tonight... only one person came to mind."

Ugh. There he goes again, saying shit that makes you forget your worth for like three seconds.

I tried to hide my smile, but my cheeks betrayed me. I could feel the heat rising. This was dangerous. I didn't do stuff like that. I don't do late-night car talks. I don't do cozy confessions and secret tea sessions.

But for some reason... with him, I wanted to.

I turned fully in my seat, cup resting on my thigh.

"So..." I said, my voice just above a whisper, "what's on your mind?"

9

Kross

I don't do parked conversations. I don't do Dubai strawberries and curated tea. I damn sure don't sit in cars and spill my childhood like I'm on The Montel Williams Show. But there I was... looking at her like she was my new favorite habit.

Something about her made me wanna do shit I'd never done before. Made me wanna be known. So I did it.

"You should already know but my full name's Krossli Givelle."

She looked at me over her tea, one brow raised. "Givelle? That sounds like a candle scent."

I smirked. "Keep playing and I'll light your ass up like one, too."

She laughed and sipped again.

"I'm thirty-three. Favorite color is navy blue. Favorite food? Cajun pasta, heavy on the sausage, light on the judgment."

She blinked. "Okay, Big Back."

"I grew up in a two-parent home. Real southern. My mom is a lot like you."

That got her attention.

"She's sweet as pie," I said, "but didn't play. Especially with my daddy. Like, she'd serve him a plate then cuss him out over it. They never hid the real from us, either. I saw the good days, and I saw the days where my daddy had to sleep in the truck."

I laughed, but it wasn't funny. Just true.

"It taught me early that love ain't perfect. Some days, that shit is draining. Some days, it straight up hurts. But it's real. And I always wanted that... even though I didn't think I'd ever get it. You don't come across strong ass women like my mama no more."

Rivah tilted her head with a sly grin. "Your mama sounds like my type of lady. Is she single..."

I laughed. "Girl...."

I looked at the cup in my hand, steam rising like truth. "She ain't always been like that, though. My pops made some dumbass decisions when they were young, and instead of letting that shit break her, she made a believer outta him. Now he eatin' out her damn hand. And I'm talkin' both hands, all ten fingers—hell, maybe a toe if she said so."

Rivah was grinning, but I could tell she was listening. Really listening.

"She's the reason anything he got now exists. My dad might've had the vision, but she was the blueprint. And she doesn't let him forget it, either. Some men hate that kinda woman. I respect it. I know what she went through. You gotta love someone with your whole soul to stay after the storm—and even more to rebuild the whole house after."

Rivah looked down at her cup. Her smile softened.

"I ain't have that," she said quietly. "With my mom dying the way she did, I always say that even in the womb, I was extra. Like, she saw what was coming and said "nah I'm good."

I didn't say anything. Just watched the way she said it like it was a joke, but I heard the crack in her voice.

She caught herself quick, sipping her tea and clearing her throat. "Anyway."

"I have three brothers," I said, picking the mood up. "All our names start with K. My pops kept my mama pregnant like it was a job—back to back to back. But, she handled it like a pro."

Rivah laughed. "That's cute as hell. I love that. I was an only child. People always say that means you're spoiled. And maybe. But it's also lonely. You start talking to yourself, and next thing you know, you're arguing with your alter ego about who left the fridge open."

"Not the alter ego catching strays."

She reached over and punched my arm playfully, smiling big.

I looked at her. Like, really looked. "I like you."

She squinted. "You drunk?"

"Nah. I'm serious. You don't have to say it back—I ain't one of them." I leaned in a little closer. "I also ain't the type to get scared off easily. So, even if you ignore me tomorrow? I'm pulling the fuck up. You can write me off, block me, say your little quotes about 'soft era' and 'no access,' and I'm still pulling up."

I grinned. "A restraining order is cute too, but it won't stop me."

Rivah raised an eyebrow and leaned back with her arms folded tight under her chest.

"Well, since you out here spilling all your government secrets," she said, smirking, "I need to know if you got a lil' girlfriend. You've been in my face a whole lot, so I just need to know if I should stay ready. 'Cause I'm sure there's some woman out there ready to die behind that dick."

"And if you married?" She pointed a finger dead at me. "Go ahead and call your parents now and say your goodbyes. 'Cause I don't even play with God like that. I will literally kill you."

I shook my head, grinning. "Damn. Are you always this warm and welcoming?"

"Only on Tuesdays," she said, sipping her tea like she hadn't just threatened to commit a felony.

I put my cup down and turned to face her, serious now. "I've been single for a few years. No girlfriend. I had a... constant situation."

She side-eyed me. "A what?"

"A woman. Technically a friend, but she went with me to work events, weddings, all that. She looked good on my arm. Didn't ask too many questions. It worked. Until it didn't."

Rivah leaned in, studying me. "You still fuck her?"

I didn't flinch. "We did. From time to time. But since you? Nah. I've been ghosting her."

She blinked, then smirked. "Mmhm. Sure."

"I'm serious."

"I guess," she said with a shrug. "You can do what you want. Because I'mma do what I want, too."

That made something in me snap just a little.

"Nah. I don't like that."

She leaned closer, teasing now. "You don't have to like it, baby. My body doesn't come with a deed. No one owns me. Not a man, not a title, and sure as hell not a nut. Men gotta understand that."

I stared at her. The corner of her mouth curled into a smug smile like she thought she had me in check.

I leaned in slow, my voice dropping low and even. "Rivah. Look me in the eye and tell me you really believe that shit after what we do. After how you look at me... how you open up and let me wreck every inch of you."

She bit her lip but didn't move.

"Say it again," I said, voice rough. "Say that no one owns you. Say that and mean it."

She laughed. Soft. Nervous. But she didn't say it again.

"Exactly."

I leaned back, arms spread wide over the seat. "You can keep playing power games if that makes you feel in control. But we both know the truth."

"And what's that?"

"You want to give it up," I said. "But not just to anybody. Just to me. Because I make you feel seen... and safe. And that's the scariest shit of all."

She narrowed her eyes. I could tell I was getting too close. Too real.

She took one last sip of her tea and then turned toward me, licking her lips like she was choosing her next words carefully.

"You are so damn confident," she said with a cocky smile. "But just make sure you got your blood pressure medicine on standby if you plan on fucking with me."

I laughed, low and deep in my chest. "You threatening to be a health hazard now?"

She leaned in, her voice all sugar and sin. "Baby, I am the hazard."

I shook my head, tongue pressed to the inside of my cheek, trying not to let her see how much that turned me on.

"That's alright," I said, voice dropping as I looked her over. "I've survived worse. But you?" I leaned in just close enough to make her breath hitch. "You keep playing with me, and it's gon' be your legs needing prescriptions for strength recovery."

She blinked, blushed... and bit her lip.

Checkmate. But I didn't even need to say it.

Because the silence said it for me.

10

Rivah

The last twenty minutes of the school day felt like trying to swim through peanut butter. I was tired. My kids were tired. And yet, there we were, deep into another lesson on the human body.

"Alright, class," I said, leaning against my desk with my bottle of sparkling water like it was a wine glass. "Let's talk about digestion."

Teelamiyah raised her hand, dramatic as always. "Miss R, why we always gotta talk about what the body does and does not like... how to keep it cute?"

I tilted my head at her. "Baby, ain't nothing cute about constipation. That's how y'all end up in the nurse's office, bent over like old men at a BBQ. Y'all need fiber and you need to hydrate. Ain't no TikTok dance gon' save you from a backed-up gut."

The whole class snickered and I saw little Jaden raise his hand slowly like he was scared of the answer. "So like... when we poop, is it like... our stomach dying?"

I blinked. "No, baby. That's your body letting go of the past. Literally. It's self-care."

Alani whispered to her neighbor, "That's deep."

I kept going. "Your body has one job — keep you alive. And if you treat it right, it'll do just that. But if you go around eating hot Cheetos at 7am and drinking soda instead of water, don't be shocked when your stomach starts fighting for its life."

"Like Teelamiyah last week," someone whispered.

"EXACTLY," I said, pointing to her like she was the sponsored example.

She rolled her eyes. "Whatever. At least I don't fart during reading time."

"OKAY, that's enough," I said, clapping my hands. "Y'all homework is to drink at least two bottles of water and write one paragraph about what happens when you don't. And I swear if I get one single paper that says 'you die,' I'm giving you an F just out of laziness."

The bell rang and I was halfway into the motion of flopping into my chair when I remembered to check my phone — four missed calls and five texts from Vane.

I sighed dramatically and unlocked my phone.

> **Vane:** Bitch answer.
>
> I know you see me calling.
>
> IT'S ABOUT YOUR BLOG
>
> Not joking.
>
> Answer. The. Damn. Phone.

I stared at the screen, my stomach doing a weird little twist. Something told me this wasn't about tea or nails. I grabbed my bag and headed to the hallway, calling her back.

"Girl, what now?" I asked, halfway teasing.

"Bitch, one of your blog posts is going viral. Like—viral viral. I'm talking all the major tea pages, even the ones that mix memes with mental illness," Vane said.

I sucked my teeth. "Okay? And the problem is?"

"The problem is alot." she echoed, already sounding worked up.

"Girl, that's great news! More traction to my page, more affiliate links getting clicked, and before I know it, I'll be working part-time at this ghetto lil elementary. Bitch, buy me a celebratory cake!"

"No!" she snapped. "Not that kind of viral. Not a cute repost with a heart emoji. I'm saying this could be investigative thread type viral. Screenshots. Comments. Niggas in the comments saying 'I think this about me.'"

I paused, still not catching the urgency. "Okay... and?"

"It's the one from months ago. The one I told you to delete. The one with too many damn details."

My stomach dropped a little. "...Which one?"

"Number 11."

I burst out laughing. "Vane, please. You know how many people are missing that tooth? You're acting like I used his government name."

"You practically did," she said. "And since you conveniently forgot, allow me to refresh your memory."

I could hear her scrolling, dramatic as hell with her acrylic nails clacking against the screen like she was typing an obituary:

Blog Entry Title: "Tooth Be Told"

I was trying to be a better person, y'all. I really was. I had made peace with my past, saged my space, and even updated my prayer journal. But then boredom hit... and that's when Number 11 crept back in.

I talked to Number 11 on FaceTime. He was smooth, funny, and kept the camera angle real tight. I ain't think nothin' of it—until the day I pulled up and this man grinned at me in person, and all I could see was gum and trauma. Baby, he had one missing side tooth. The one that is numbered as 11, and it was in the exact spot where your tongue automatically goes when you're trying to be sexy. That poor tongue was lost. Just air and bad decisions over there.

Now, did I leave? No. Because I'm not a rude person. Also, I was already shaved and wearing good panties. So, I figured, at least let me get my coochie kissed and go home. Don't judge me, judge ya mama.

And yes—he ate. And to my surprise, it was good. I'm talking 'slightly redeemed himself' good. But, what I didn't forget was that this man had a birthmark shaped like the state of Florida right above his dick. I'm not exaggerating. The dick itself was giving... *average traveler*—not quite long enough for international travel, but might make it to the next state over on a good day.

Let's talk red flags, because this man had a warehouse full.

First of all, this fool sat across from me and told me that if he ever got married, his wife would sign a prenup because *"he is the prize."*

Sir, you live in a two-bedroom apartment with three gaming chairs and one butter knife. Please be for real.

He also said he'd never go 100% for a woman. "It's 50/50 over here. And if you can't match what I bring, you don't deserve me."

Match what? Your Snapback collection and a dream?

Anyway, against my better judgment, we got it poppin'. And y'all... I should've stayed home and organized my spice cabinet.

Every time I started to moan or rotate my hips, he'd pause and whisper, "You're doing too much. Chill out. Just take it slow."

Boy, if you don't take this barely-there dick so I can go home. I can't even get one good back arch before you huffin' and actin' like I'm a rodeo bull.

The only thing that stayed hard was my disappointment.

Final rating? 3/10. He gets 2 points for oral and 1 for keeping his socks on so I wouldn't have to see his feet.

Would I repeat? Absolutely not. He was the type of man who'd ask for a plate but wouldn't help bring groceries in. The type that got a podcast mic but no job.

Sometimes, ladies, the red flags aren't just waving—they're forming a damn parade.

So here's your reminder:

You are not asking for too much. He's just offering too little.

Know your worth. Ladies, if he got the nerve to be missing a tooth and talking down on women—just know, you're not asking for too much... you're just talking to somebody who ain't even got all his body parts.

Vane finished reading the blog post dramatically like she was doing spoken word at a poetry slam. I tried my best not to laugh.

"Well, if he reads it," I said with a shrug, "he'll definitely know I'm talking about him."

"Rivah..."

"Girl, who cares?" I said, completely unbothered.

"I just don't know where I went wrong with you."

"Probably somewhere around 10th grade," I said, slipping on my sunglasses. "I've been like this."

I walked to the parking lot and I got into my car. I hadn't even closed the door good before my text tone went off. I tilted the phone and immediately grinned.

"Hold on," I said, taking the phone off speaker, "he just touched down."

"Father Abraham?"

"Who else?"

She laughed. "Whew, child. Not the patriarch himself."

Father Abraham. The man, the myth, the multiple birth certificates. We'd been doing our dance for five years. He worked overseas, looked like an R&B song with a beard, and had manners that would make your granny approve. But... he also had situations.

Two sets of twins. By two different women. Back to back like Drake singles.

As fine and sweet as he was, I knew better than to volunteer to be a full-time bonus mama to four toddlers and a circus of baby mamas who stayed online throwing shade at each other. I liked him too much to grow to hate him. So we kept it cute, casual, and respectful.

I called him Father Abraham because—well—he had many sons. And always possibly a daughter or two on the way.

He sent me the name of a restaurant and a time. No words. Just location and vibes.

I smiled and looked at Vane.

"I'm headed home to get ready," I said, sliding my phone into my bag. "Long lost friend wants to wine and dine me."

"Long lost?" she asked.

"Yeah. Lost in the sauce. But he always finds his way back."

And so do I. Just long enough to eat, sip, and pretend like he ain't got a whole daycare in his DNA.

NETRA ANTIONETTE

The host barely had time to greet me before I was gliding through the restaurant, hips swaying with just enough arrogance to make a man repent. My heels clicked against the marble floor like I had a personal soundtrack, and my dress did what needed to be done — hugged my curves like it missed me and slid against my skin like it had secrets to keep.

It wasn't even red, but it had bad decisions written all over it.

The second I stepped into the main dining area, I saw him.

Father Abraham.

Sitting at a table tucked in the back, champagne already sweating in the bucket like it knew what night it was about to be.

He stood up as soon as he saw me, like always. That man was Southern manners and deep strokes wrapped in a dark chocolate package built like he fixed tractors on Monday and bodies on Friday.

Muscular. Country. Hands that could rebuild a car engine or grip the back of your thighs while whispering Bible verses.

He walked over, kissed my cheek, and pulled me in with one hand sliding down to the small of my back — skin to skin. His lips brushed against my ear as he whispered,

"Damn, baby girl."

I smirked and pulled back slowly. "Let's make it through dinner first. This is one of my favorite restaurants and I'm not about to skip my meal."

He chuckled and licked his lips. "Aight then, as long as you agree to be my dessert."

We slid into our seats and the candlelight between us flickered like it knew the tension was about to get sinful.

Now don't get me wrong — Father Abraham wasn't better than Kross.

Not at all. But before Kross, He was the man I thought about when I didn't want company but my rose toy was fully charged.

He talked like sex, smelled like leather and warm bourbon, and looked at me like he'd been praying for my body all Ramadan.

He was a gentleman to the world and a professional back-blower in private. That's what made him dangerous and irresistible.

As we ordered and settled in, his eyes never left mine. Not even when the waitress poured the wine.

"So how long are you in town this time?" I asked, twirling my glass slowly.

"Just a few days," he said, voice low and deep, "but I'm tryna make every one count."

And the way he said it made my legs cross under the table involuntarily.

The waitress had just walked away with our orders when my phone buzzed on the table.

> **Kross:** Where are you at?

I smirked immediately. Didn't even bother hiding it and took a sip of wine before replying.

> I'm grown.

Not even ten seconds passed.

> I told you, when I come, you open the door.

I laughed. This man was really full of himself tonight.

> Too bad, too sad. I'm not home.

The dots danced as he typed.

> Where are you?

I grinned as I typed back slow.

> For me to know and for you to find out.

I could practically feel the heat through the phone when his reply came back.

> I see what kinda games you playing. Tell that nigga he got 15 minutes to get up and go before I lay you on that dinner table and eat your pussy in front of him. Show him who it really belongs to.

I bit my lip and clenched my thighs under the table.

Goddamn.

"Everything okay?" Father Abraham asked, his tone calm but curious as he watched me with those deep brown eyes. He took a sip of his bourbon, but I could tell he caught the shift in my energy.

I glanced down at the message again and shook my head with a little laugh I couldn't hold in.

> **Me (to Kross):** LMAO, yeah okay.

Then I dropped my phone face down on the table and leaned in toward Abraham, placing my elbow on the linen and my chin in my hand, all sweet and seductive.

"It's just someone who wants to be relevant," I said with a little eye roll. "Now... what were you saying before I got distracted by desperation?"

He laughed, but I didn't. Not fully.

Because even though I was sitting across from a man I used to think was my safest bet...

I couldn't stop thinking about the man threatening to flip this whole dinner table over just to remind me who really had my body on lock.

And that shit turned me on way more than I would ever admit.

The waitress had just placed our appetizers down—some bougie shit Abraham ordered that looked like art on a plate. Ahi tuna tartare with edible flowers and something green I couldn't pronounce. He was already leaning in, flashing that country-boy grin like he knew I was seconds away from melting.

"So when you gon' stop playing and let me fly you out to Dubai?" he asked, voice deep and smooth like warm honey. "Let you see what imported pleasure feels like."

I laughed. "I can't go out the country with a man who has enough kids to start his own national anthem."

Our waitress leaned over discreetly and whispered in my ear, "There's a guest at the front asking for you by name."

My whole face shifted.

I turned slightly, eyes scanning the hostess stand.

And there was **Kross.**

Standing there in all his dark-skin glory, black tee hugging his biceps, his gold chain glinting under the restaurant's lighting.

I smirked to myself before turning back to Abraham. "Excuse me for a second."

I stood up slow, real slow. If Kross wanted to act bold, he was gonna get a show. I let my hips sway just a little more than usual—knowing Father Abraham was watching me leave and Kross was watching me approach. One looking at everything behind me. The other looking at everything he wanted back in front of him.

Double homicide.

When I finally made it to him, I folded my arms and smiled real sweet. "How can I help you?"

Kross didn't miss a beat. "You can get your shit and leave with me."

I tilted my head, amused. "How the hell did you even find me?"

His lips curled into that cocky grin. "Your taste has never been cheap, and I know people who know people."

I raised an eyebrow. "So, what I'm hearing is... you stalkin' now?"

He stepped a little closer, voice low and lethal. "Nah. I'm not a stalker. But when I mark something as mine, I don't like nobody coming behind me."

I almost gasped. Not because I was scared.

Because I was wet.

I leaned in with a smirk and whispered, "Have a nice night, Kross. I'll be sure to think about you when his lips are all over me."

Then I turned, giving him the same show I gave walking up.

Only this time, I knew both their eyes were on me—and I didn't care one damn bit.

I sat down like I hadn't just been summoned by my favorite toxic temptation at the front of the restaurant. Abraham leaned back, sipping his drink.

"These little men of yours really don't know who run the calendar, huh?" he said, playful.

I lifted my fork. "Sir, don't flatter yourself. My rotation doesn't stop when you come home. You just got a good time slot."

But just as I went to stab into the appetizer, my fork disappeared.

I looked up, and Kross was standing over the table.

He ate my bite of food like it was his meal. "Yeah, this is alright... but you should've ordered the scallop risotto. Never pick pretty over pleasure."

I didn't get to respond before he turned to Abraham and stuck his hand out. "Name's Kross."

Abraham moved to respond, but Kross cut him off without missing a beat.

"Doesn't matter. She won't remember your name by the time she's screaming mine again."

CHILE.

I felt my coochie blink.

He turned back to me and lowered his voice, but not enough because everyone within five tables heard him.

"I told you, if you didn't leave, I'd pull up and eat your pussy in front of whoever had the balls to sit across from you. You really brought this pretty little plate to the table, but left the feast behind."

The table behind me gasped. I heard a 'Jesus!' from somebody's auntie.

Abraham blinked. "Yo... I ain't even know y'all was like that. I'm not tryna fight behind no pussy, fam. She grown."

"Exactly," Kross said, leaning over my shoulder now, whispering it, but making sure everyone could still hear. "She grown. And that grown ass pussy? That shit sacred. That shit is art. And I don't play about it."

He kissed my neck slow, soft, and nasty. Then looked me dead in my face.

"I worship that pussy. That little pretty pussy you got that moans when I just look at it. And you out here letting weak ass hands touch it like it ain't the holy grail? Like it doesn't deserve to be on a pedestal with roses and rainwater? Nah. That shit mine. It needs me. You need me."

I blinked right along with the whole restaurant.

The waiter at table six dropped a damn wine glass.

Abraham cleared his throat. "Aye look... I ain't even know she was yours like that. She ain't say none of that."

Kross didn't even look at him. He looked at me.

"She didn't have to. Her body did."

And I felt my thighs betray me.

Then he kissed my forehead.

"Let's go."

He walked off slow, like he knew I'd follow him. And God help me... I did.

But not before I looked Abraham dead in the face and said, "Your dick cute, but not special. Stop making twins and go get a vasectomy. The community thanks you."

I grabbed my drink, raised it in cheers, then dropped it—*oops*—right into his lap.

"Oh damn, my bad. Slippery when wet."

I strutted out, heels clacking, ass swaying, coochie ready for Kross.

11

Kross

I slipped the valet a folded hundred and a card with an address scribbled on the back.

"Take her car here. Leave the keys with the front lobby. And make sure there's not a single scratch on it."

The kid nodded fast like he just met a cartel boss. "Yessir, I got it."

I turned toward Rivah—still standing there looking like temptation in heels and attitude. I opened the passenger side door and pointed to the seat. No words needed.

She crossed her arms. "I can't drive my own car home now? What is this—kidnapping?"

I looked her up and down slow. Deliberate. "No. This is me being responsible... because where we're going and after what we do, you won't be in any condition to drive."

That made her blink, but she didn't say no. She slid into the seat like she didn't want to admit she liked being told what to do.

I closed the door behind her, walked around to my side, and got in. I hit the 'Home' button on the screen.

Her head tilted when she saw.

I looked at her—calm, but direct.

"We're not going to your house."

NETRA ANTIONETTE

We pulled into my driveway and I noticed the way her eyes wandered—taking everything in like she was trying not to be impressed. I hit the button and the garage door eased up, revealing the lineup inside.

She leaned toward the window and muttered, "Damn. You really wasn't lying about living in *The Toast*."

I smirked. "I'll never lie to you, Rivah Renée Banks."

Her head snapped in my direction when I said her full name, like she wasn't expecting me to have it ready like that. I got out, walked around to her side, and opened the door.

She stepped out in those heels that made her legs look even longer. Her eyes bounced between the vintage '67 Mustang, the all-black Audi, and the candy red classic Impala sitting like it belonged in a photo shoot.

"Okay, Fancy Pants," she said, lips curled into a grin. "Garage lookin' like a whole showroom."

I chuckled, locking the car behind her. "I like classic cars. I like luxury. Nothing wrong with that." I paused and looked at her. "I like you too, right?"

She raised a brow but nodded slowly. "Yeah, you're right."

She didn't say anything, but the way she walked past me with that little sway in her hips told me everything I needed to know.

She stepped inside like she belonged there, like this wasn't her first time walking through million-dollar homes. Her eyes didn't even widen—just flicked over everything with cool interest as she walked further in, her heels clicking across my hardwood floors.

She took in the clean lines of my living room, the oversized sectional, the glass art installation on the wall that looked like broken time. Her fingers brushed over the edge of the marble counter in the open kitchen.

"You got taste," she said over her shoulder. "But I already knew that because you've been trying to taste me since day one."

I smirked, leaning against the doorway with my arms folded. "Still waiting on that invite, Miss Banks."

"You got one the other night," she said, peeking down a hallway. "You just didn't know how long it was good for."

I pushed off the frame and walked up behind her. "Still valid?"

She turned toward me, that slow smile playing on her lips like she knew she was leading me into something I wouldn't come back from. "Depends."

"On what?"

"If you can handle it."

I didn't respond. I just stepped in closer, brushing a finger down her arm. "You keep talkin' like you weren't the one who was laid out breathin' like you saw Jesus the other night."

She laughed. "And you keep talkin' like you weren't the one stuck in the moment."

"Are you done exploring?"

She tilted her head. "Not yet. But you can assist me."

"I plan to," I said watching her dress slide down her shoulders.

She didn't stop me, just let it drop. I kissed the side of her neck first. Soft. Then let my lips trail down her collarbone, across her chest. She sighed, finally faltering for a second—just long enough for me to wrap an arm around her waist and lift her off her feet.

She gasped. "What are you doing?"

"Taking what's mine. You knew what this was."

I laid her on my bed, and she looked at me with that look. The one she tries to mask with attitude and sarcasm, but I saw her. I always did. And I was going to make sure she felt seen.

I took my time.. Letting my eyes eat up every curve like it was my last meal. She smirked, but I caught the shift in her breathing. The way her thighs pressed together when I pulled my shirt over my head.

"You gone keep starin', or you gone do something?" she asked, voice low, teasing.

I climbed onto the bed, slow and controlled, crawling up her like a storm coming in quiet.

"Don't rush me, Rivah. I plan to enjoy every inch of what's mine."

Her breath caught.

I kissed her shoulder first. Then her neck. Then that soft spot under her jaw that makes her moan loud. My lips trailed down, warm and slow. My tongue teased one nipple, then the other, until she arched her back and gasped my name like it was the only word she knew.

"Fuck..."

"You good?" I murmured, dragging my tongue up her stomach before kissing her again—deep and open.

She nodded, but I didn't stop to let her answer.

When I slid inside her, she cried out. *"Kross!"* Like that. Loud and breathless. I gripped her hips and gave her every inch. No holding back. I wanted her to feel me for days.

"Just like that," I growled. "You feel what you do to me? You hear it?"

The sounds of our bodies—wet, wild, unapologetic—filled the room like music. I looked into her eyes, and I swear she was close to crying.

"You think you in control?" I whispered, lips brushing hers. "You think this pussy yours?"

She started to speak, and I cut her off by flipping her on her stomach and dragging her to the edge of the bed by her waist. She looked back at me, dazed, mouth parted. I slapped her ass once—light, but enough to make her gasp.

"You're mine, Rivah. All of you."

I bent over her, kissed her back, and pushed in again, this time slower, deeper.

"I want you to feel this in your chest. In your fucking throat."

She clawed at the sheets, her legs shaking.

Then I did what she didn't expect—I slowed down. Got soft with it. Kissed her shoulder again. "I want to make love to the parts of your nobody's ever touched."

She whimpered. Whispered my name like a prayer.

So I flipped her again, made her ride me. Her curls wild, her hands on my chest, her body taking every stroke like she was built for it.

She leaned down, bit my lip, whispered, "You gone make me fall for you, acting like this."

"You already have."

I let her take over—watching her bounce, ride, fall apart on my dick like she wanted to ruin me.

Then I grabbed her waist and met her stroke for stroke, fucking up into her so hard her moans turned into screams.

I felt her start to come again, her walls pulsing, eyes rolling—and I didn't pull out.

I came deep. Hot. Heavy. Every ounce of me spilled into her like a man who already knew he'd never want another woman again.

She collapsed beside me, breathless.

I picked her up, one arm under her thighs, the other on her back.

She blinked up at me, dazed. "Kross—"

"Shower," I said, carrying her like she weighed nothing.

"I can't even feel my legs," she whispered, giggling.

"You won't feel anything if I stay in this bed with you," I said, setting her down in my bathroom. "And baby..."

I turned the water on, stepped into the steam behind her, pressed her against the glass.

"...we're not done."

I stepped into the shower with her body still wrapped around me.

Her back hit the tile, and her arms tightened around my neck. She whispered something soft and breathy, but I didn't hear it. I felt it. Her nails dragging along my shoulders, the way her thighs locked around my waist like she wasn't done either.

"Are you sure you got anything left?" I teased, pressing my forehead to hers. She smiled through swollen lips. "Try me."

So I did.

Right there, water pouring down our skin, her body pressed between me and the wall—I held her up with one arm and fed her everything I had left with the other. Deep strokes that made her whimper and beg, that had her moaning into my mouth like she couldn't believe she was still climbing.

And when she came again, she damn near collapsed.

I held her tighter. Kissed her shoulder. Slowed my pace until I gave her the last of me, buried so deep she shook all over.

After that, I didn't say a word. Just kissed her temple and set her gently down.

She leaned against the tile, trying to catch her breath, and I reached for the body wash. I lathered up my hands and ran them over her body. Not like a man trying to rush, but like one trying to memorize.

She watched me quietly and a little dazed. Her long lashes heavy over sleepy eyes.

When I got to her legs, she lifted her foot like she trusted me with every part of her.

I rinsed her off, then turned the water down so it wouldn't burn while I washed myself. She didn't say a word—just sat on the little bench in the shower, legs curled under her, watching me. Eyes low. Tired, but trying not to show it.

I cut the water off and grabbed a towel. She didn't even move when I picked her up again. Just sighed into my shoulder like she could fall asleep right there.

I laid her on the bed, kissed her forehead. She sat up, fighting to look alert.

"I need to go home," she mumbled, voice soft and groggy. "It's Thursday. I have work in the morning."

She was already grabbing her things—heels, phone.

But I took them out of her hands and set them back down.

"What are you doing?" she asked, raising a brow.

I pulled the blanket back, slid into the bed, and patted the space beside me.

"Lay down."

"Kross, I'm serious. I can't just stay—"

"You can. And you will."

"I have a job. I don't just take random days off—"

"You barely ever take days off at all." I looked at her, dead in the eyes. "Call in, Rivah. Tell them you'll see them Monday. Or I'll pull up to your job tomorrow morning in a black hoodie and cause a bigger scene than I did at that damn restaurant."

She narrowed her eyes. "Kross, be so fucking for real"

"Try me," I said, pulling the cover back even more. "Be the reason I go viral."

She rolled her eyes, but she got in the bed anyway. That mouth of hers wouldn't stop, but her body already told the truth.

I handed her the phone and raised an eyebrow. "Go 'head. Make the call."

She sighed dramatically. "You are a menace."

"And yet, you love it here."

She grinned despite herself, pressed the phone to her ear, and when a lady picked up, I leaned over and whispered.

"Tell them you'll see them Monday, baby. That's all they need to know."

12

Rivah

The smell hit me first. Buttery. Savory. Coffee-brewing rich.

I blinked into the morning light spilling through the curtains, confused because… I knew I smelled food, but Kross's arm was still draped heavily across my waist.

Wait.

I turned slowly.

The man was still asleep behind me. Breathing deep and peaceful like he wasn't the one who turned my damn body into mashed potatoes. His legs tangled with mine. His chest pressed to my back. And we were still naked.

My phone was face down on the side table. I picked it up.

9:04 A.M.

I damn near dropped it. Nine? I hadn't slept in that late since before my last heartbreak.

I laid there for a second, staring at the ceiling like it might explain what the hell was going on with me. I hadn't shared a bed with a man in years. Not even Father Abraham stayed past 3AM. I might've borrowed his body for some stress relief, but I was always gone before the birds could gossip.

"Kross," I whispered, nudging him. "Why do I smell food?"

He kissed the top of my head without even opening his eyes. "I scheduled my chef to come in."

His voice was all low and raspy like he didn't just ruin my equilibrium the night before.

I sat up slowly, grabbing the sheet and wrapping it around myself, even though the man had been inside every part of me. He reached over and pulled one side of the sheet down, just enough to let my nipple peek out and then he latched onto it, warm tongue and soft lips like it belonged to him.

"Kross," I moaned and swatted at his head. "Stop playin'. Let's go eat so you can take you home."

He looked up at me, unfazed. "You're not going anywhere. My brothers and their girls are on the way over for breakfast anyway."

I blinked. "I'm sorry... what?"

"You heard me."

I blinked again. "I don't even have decent clothes."

He smirked and pointed toward the door near the bathroom. "Taken care of."

I threw the covers back, walked barefoot across his damn hardwood floors like a woman possessed, and opened the door. And almost passed out.

I walked in and the lights automatically flipped on. Racks and racks. Tags still on. Everything in my size. Dresses, jeans, cropped sweaters, two kinds of shoes for every look. Designer labels like it was a pop-up boutique.

I turned around slowly, staring at him with my mouth open. "Krossli Givelle, what in the emotionally manipulative hell is this?"

He grinned like the devil himself. "Just a few essentials. I didn't want to fill it completely. Thought I'd leave the rest to you."

"You know this is insane, right?"

"You say that," he said, stretching as he got out the bed, still naked like his dick didn't need warning labels. "But you're smiling like a woman about to max out my card."

I tried to hold my face, I swear I did—but the smile snuck out anyway.

"Yeah, well," I muttered. "I am crazy. So again, don't forget your blood pressure medicine fuckin' with me."

He laughed and kissed my cheek. "I got it already in the nightstand. Let's go eat."

NETRA ANTIONETTE

I was sitting at Kross's kitchen table, sipping coffee like I belonged there, which was crazy because I never did no shit like that. We were deep in a conversation about why men who wear slides with socks feel the need to walk like they're dragging both regret and entitlement across the floor, when the front door flung open like a Tyler Perry play.

Two tall, chocolate, copy-and-paste examples of God showing out walked in loud as hell—laughing, pushing each other like kids, and smelling like cologne, luxury, and trouble. All three of them had the same strong jaws, deep-set eyes, and broad shoulders that made you reconsider your birth control.

"Damn," I whispered, sipping my coffee like it was tea.

Kross stood up, smirking. "Rivah, that's Kairo, the oldest. And that fool there is Kordai—the baby."

"Nice to meet you," Kairo said, flashing a smile that looked like it cost him a lot of heartbreak and some lawyer fees.

Kordai nodded at me with a grin that was too damn confident for someone that fine at that time of hour. "So, this the one got my brother on his best behavior?"

I didn't respond. I just blinked slow like a cat and took another sip.

They sat down like it was just a regular day, and Kross casually asked, "Where's Khloe?"

Kairo sucked his teeth and leaned back, clearly annoyed. "Man, she got called in on some emergency. She at work."

Before anyone could respond, the doorbell rang again—but that was just a formality because the front door swung open right after, followed by chaos.

Click clack. Click clack.

"I TOLD YOU STOP FUCKIN PLAYING WITH ME, KENDRIX!"

We all turned toward the front hall like it was a live episode of Cheaters.

Kairo shook his head, already grinning. "That's Niv. Coming in talking shit to Kendrix like always."

All the brothers busted out laughing like this was routine.

Kross just leaned over and whispered in my ear, "Prepare yourself."

Because if that was the intro... I already knew the family brunch was about to be everything but peaceful.

We were wrapping up breakfast and my stomach was full, but the real main course had been the entertainment.

"Why you lookin' at me like that?" Niv asked Kendrix, tilting her head like she was ready to throw hands.

"I ain't even doin' nun," he said, wiping his mouth with his napkin and shrugging with all the fake innocence of a man who absolutely did something.

Niv sat her mimosa down. "Don't act stupid. You let that hoe sit in your lap last night like you forgot that I'm crazy as fuck."

"She tripped! Slipped on the edge of the stage and just happened to land there."

"Oh, so she tripped?" Niv raised a brow, her voice calm but her energy was pre-charged for chaos. "Well, I must've slipped when I slapped her ass too, huh? My bad."

Kendrix chuckled, trying to act unbothered. "Here you go with the dramatics."

"I will be dramatic," she said, turning fully in her chair. "If I see a bitch blink too slow in your direction again, I'ma show her what a real blackout looks like. Keep playin' with me, baby."

The table went quiet for half a second before Kross clapped his hands together, loud and rushed. "Alright, alright—yo, I wanna show y'all something in the basement real quick."

Kairo and Kordai stood up fast, like they'd seen this show before and knew to exit stage left. Kendrix smirked and leaned down to kiss Niv on the cheek.

"Baby, the nerd wants to show us somethin'. I'll be back."

"Don't be long," she muttered, fixing her hoop earring like it doubled as a weapon.

He turned to me with a lazy grin. "Nice to meet you, Rivah. You have that sweet face, but I can see it—you one of them, too."

I just smiled like I wasn't sure what the hell that meant but felt seen anyway.

The guys disappeared toward the basement, and suddenly, it was just me and Niv sitting at the table with empty plates, champagne glasses, and a whole lot of unspoken thoughts.

She looked at me, chin resting in her palm. "So...you fuckin' him or nah?"

I choked on air. "Excuse me?"

She grinned. "I'm just sayin'—you sittin' here in designer with your hair in a bun. I know that look."

I laughed, heat crawling up my neck. "Girl."

"What?" she sipped her mimosa. "You ain't gotta tell me. I can tell. And it's okay—Kross looks like the type to make you call outta work and forget your morals."

I shook my head, laughing too hard to disagree. "You're insane."

"No," she said, licking her lips. "I'm honest. Welcome to the family, sis. It's ghetto, but the dick good and the brunch slaps."

"Family?" I raised my brows and leaned back in my chair, sipping the last of my mimosa. "I don't know about all that. This shit was pretty much forced. I just came to get my pussy ate and back broke and woke up with breakfast and demands to meet the family like I signed a contract or something."

Niv burst out laughing, smacking the table. "Oh bitch, same. That sounds just like me and Kendrix."

She sat up a little, mimosa in one hand, nails catching the light like she had stories in every sparkle. "Well, let me properly introduce myself and catch you up since that dickhead of a man you got didn't."

She extended her hand all playful and bougie. "My name's Niveah, but everybody calls me Niv. If you ever hear him yell 'Shut up, Niv!' that's me."

I chuckled and shook her hand. "Rivah. Nice to meet you for real."

"You married?" I asked, curious.

She looked at me like I told her I wanted to live on a prayer and expired milk. "Hell naw!" she said loud as hell, making me try not to choke on my own breath.

"I wouldn't dare," she added with a dramatic eye roll. "Me and Kendrix shared one night. One. And he has been actin' like I came from his rib ever since."

I laughed. "So what, you like him?"

"I mean, yeah. I love his hoe ass. But don't tell him that or he'll get cocky."

I smirked, already liking her chaotic energy. She leaned in with a wink.

"I'm a midnight ballerina," she said, like she was telling me a family recipe. "One of the most elite and exclusive men's clubs in Stonehaven. Think velvet stages, cigar smoke, jazz so smooth it'll make you ovulate. I only dance for select clientele—top shelf only. Got a couple high-rolling sponsors who keep my bills paid and my closet disrespectful."

She leaned back, sipped, and pointed her nail at me. "But keep that between me and you. If Kendrix finds out, I'll have to fake my death."

"You wild as hell," I said, still laughing.

"He wild, too," she added. "He got one more time to pull some dumb shit and I'm out. He already thinks we go together, and we don't."

"That must be in their blood," I said, rolling my eyes. "Kross does the same thing. Acting like I belong to him just cause I let him rearrange my uterus."

"See?" she snapped her fingers. "That's how they get you. Dick you down real good and suddenly they your man, your daddy, and your landlord."

We both cracked up, the kind of laughter that leaves your chest light and your eyes watery.

Niv leaned in again. "He asked you to be his girlfriend?"

"No."

She shrugged. "Then you ain't shit."

I spit-laughed. "Girl, you are unhinged."

She grinned wide. "And accurate. I don't play that shit."

As soon as the room got quiet again, I leaned back in my chair and raised an eyebrow at Niv.

"Okay... so, who the hell is Khloe?"

Niv smirked and rolled her eyes like she'd been waiting for me to ask. "Oh, that's Kairo's wife. She basically grew up with them. Childhood bestie turned wifey. Real storybook shit. Kairo runs the family's real estate empire, like a true oldest son—got the weight of the world on his back and the ego to match."

She popped a grape into her mouth and kept going, unbothered. "Khloe's a real estate attorney. Smart as hell, fine, polished. He loves her dirty-ass draws, but let me tell you—that doesn't mean shit when it comes to a man doing what he is supposed to do."

I blinked. "You saying he—?"

"I'm saying," she cut in, eyes wide with drama, "I think she's cheating on him. Finally. And honestly? Good for her." She laughed like she already had her popcorn ready for the fallout.

I shook my head, smirking. "And Kross?"

She shrugged and leaned back, lifting her glass. "Second born. The smart one. They always call him nerdy, but they lowkey worship that man. Be calling him about taxes, contracts, baby mama drama—like he is the family oracle."

I laughed. "Yeah, that makes sense."

"Now, unfortunately," she continued with a dramatic sigh, "I ended up with the third born. Kendrix. He's a drama queen with a beard. Owns a chain of upscale cigar lounges and runs an underground poker club in the city."

She cut her eyes at me and smirked. "You should come with me sometime. It's like 'Power' meets 'Players Club.' Very exclusive."

I raised a brow and pretended to think. "Maybe I will."

"And then there's Kordai. The baby," she added. "He just got out not too long ago. He was locked up three years for a charge he didn't even commit. I haven't seen him with a woman or heard much, so I ain't got no tea there. But from what I know, he stays low and moves quiet."

I nodded, taking it all in like I just got the Givelle family briefing. "Damn. Y'all really like a Netflix limited series."

She laughed. "And the best part? Their mama and daddy—crazy as hell. But I love them. I think I love his mama more than I love Kendrix."

I let out a laugh so hard I nearly choked. "Now see, that's wild."

Niv nodded like she meant it with her soul. "No lies detected."

"Yeah..." I said, standing and fixing my shorts, "from what I heard, she's the one to meet."

"Facts," Niv said, sipping the last of her drink.

The conversation between me and Niv had finally quieted down. I was sitting at the table scrolling on my phone, trying to look relaxed but my hands kept shaking like I had too much damn espresso and no food. I could feel her looking at me.

"You good?" she asked with a brow raised. "Your thumb twitchin' like you trying to play Candy Crush with Parkinson's."

I laughed but didn't look up. "Girl, chill."

She didn't. Of course she didn't. She leaned over fast as hell and tilted her head just enough to peek at my screen.

I didn't even have time to hide it before she gasped and smacked the table. "Bitch! I know not!"

I turned red like I got caught on stage in a school play with no lines. "It's not that—hell no. I was just—checking."

"Uh huh." She folded her arms like a concerned auntie. "Why are you on a period tracker app, Rivah?"

"Because..." I sighed and looked around like Kross might just pop up out the shadows. "Last night was our first time not using protection. My dumb ass was so into it that I didn't even realize until after. And then... I let it happen again."

I could see the spirit leave her body as she said, "Oh hell no. Come on."

"Come on where?" I asked, standing up like a guilty ass kid.

"Emergency titty-saving mission. Let's go."

We walked out the back door and around the side of the house. I saw all the brothers' cars lined up like a damn car show. But then I saw her truck. A blacked-out Range Rover sitting pretty in the corner with purple detailing. A car that said "I got my own shit but will still take your man for fun."

Niv unlocked it and climbed in like she was on a mission. She reached into her glove compartment and turned around with two packs in her hand.

She slapped them in my palm like she was passing down a family heirloom. "Two packs. The Plan B deluxe."

I blinked. "Damn, you keep them on deck?"

"Girl, I dance for billionaires and date a man who doesn't believe in pulling out. Yes, I keep them on deck."

She pointed at the pills. "I don't know how long that fine-ass terrorist is gonna keep you here, but take one now. And if he traps you in this damn house for a few more days.. Take the second one. But when you get some alone time away from him, go get on some birth control."

She paused and looked me dead in the eye. "Those Givelle men don't shoot blanks. And don't make that man a permanent part of your life until you know for sure you are ready to be stuck in the throes of emotional and parenting warfare."

I swallowed and nodded. "Damn. Noted."

"Do you have a purse?" she asked as we walked back in.

"Yeah," I said.

"Put that shit in there. They're real strict about not touching a woman's purse. That's something their mama drilled into them, so it's sacred."

I smirked. "Respect."

"It's survival," Niv said, serious as hell. "Now go on and tuck that in there like your rent money."

I smiled. "Thank you, Niv."

She waved it off and said, "Mm-hmm. I love Kendrix, but that nigga ain't done the emotional labor required to be anybody's daddy—not even a fish. So we gotta look out for each other. And if that pill doesn't work..."

She leaned in close. "Call me. We'll take a quick girls trip and hit up a fetus deletus. Your body, your choice. Fuck these niggas."

I wheezed.

Then she took my phone, opened my contacts, and typed in her name. "There. Now you got me saved. Text me if you need to fake a funeral or an alibi. I'm down."

I couldn't help but laugh. All I ever really had was Vane. But even Vane thought I was unhinged and emotionally unstable most days.

Niv? She was just as wild, reckless, and real as me—and that was exactly my vibe.

I knew I was gonna like her.

13

Kross

A few hours had passed since the noise of my brothers filled the house like a damn reunion episode. Niv and Rivah hit it off instantly—too instantly if you asked me, but I let them have their moment. After everyone left, me and Rivah knocked out for a nap that hit harder than expected. When we got up, the chef had already dipped out but left some fire finger foods in the warming tray, like he knew we'd need a little bite to come down from everything else.

We were laid out on the couch. A movie playing in the background neither of us was watching. The soft lighting gave the room a dim warmth.

I leaned forward, reaching for the throw blanket at the end of the couch when her hand stopped me.

"I can't just sit here," she said.

I looked at her, hand still hovering over mine.

"I need to ask something."

I sat back, arm slung behind her. "Alright. Shoot."

She turned, legs curled up underneath her like she was bracing herself. "What are we doing?"

I blinked. "Watching a damn movie."

She rolled her eyes. "No. What are we really doing, Kross?"

Her voice was steady, but her eyes were screaming confusion. Hurt, even. Like she was trying not to care but couldn't help that she did.

"You show up to my house whenever you want. You pull up on me mid-date like I belong to you. You bring me to your house—your real house. Not a trap house. Not a 'for fun' condo, but your house…"

Her voice cracked just a little, but she pushed through.

"You fuck me like you love me, give me a damn closet in your home with clothes that you already bought—in my size. And then you have me meeting your family like I'm somebody. So, I'm confused. I'm trying not to be. But I am. Just tell me. What the fuck are we doing?"

I leaned back, exhaled slowly, trying not to let the tightness in my chest get to me. Because the truth was—she was right.

I never did this shit. Never brought a woman home. Never made a woman fit into my space. I had properties for nights like that. Women who knew not to ask for more than what I gave. But Rivah pulled it out of me without even trying.

I looked her in the eye. "You wanna know what we're doing?"

She didn't speak. Just gave me that look that said, don't play with me.

"We're doing something I've never done before."

Her brows furrowed.

"This house? No woman's been here. I've fucked around—yeah. I've dated. Entertained. But always somewhere else. Not here. Not this bed. Not this space. Because this is mine. And you're the first woman I've ever wanted inside it."

She shifted like she was trying to process what that meant.

I continued. "You're right. I pull up when I want. I text when I want. I come get you when I want. And that's because I want you. And I don't do half-ass. Not with you."

I leaned closer.

"I gave you a closet because I plan on seeing you here more than just at night. I introduced you to my family because I feel like sometimes you understand me more than most of them do. And I fuck you like I love you because I probably do."

Her eyes locked on mine.

"I can't keep doing this," she said. "I can't just sit here and pretend."

I tilted my head. "Pretend what?"

"That this is normal. You act like I'm yours. But I don't do love. I don't do 'mine.' I don't trust it. Because love? Love hurts. And when it hurts... I have nobody to run to."

I went still. She wasn't finished.

"My mama died before I could even remember the sound of her laugh. All I know is the stories people tell me—how she was beautiful, strong, how much she loved me. But love is no good to a child who can't feel it."

She paused, but I didn't move.

"My daddy... he did his best. Military man. Disciplined. Focused. But he gave me everything. He loved me so hard, I didn't know how to break. He built me strong. Strong enough to keep going.. And that money everybody loves to talk about? The trust fund, the material things, the comfortable life he left me? That's not love. That's just silence with a price tag. That's a cold bed I go home to at night."

She looked away, but I could see her blinking hard.

"I tried love TWICE. The sweet kind. The kind they make movies about. I cooked, cleaned, prayed, sucked, submitted, supported. I did everything the internet, the podcasts, and the 'pick-me' prophets said I should. And I still got left with lies, betrayal, and a scar on my soul that I've been bandaging with situationships and ego ever since."

Her chest rose, shallow breaths filled with pain.

"I don't love because I can't afford to. Because when love fails, and it will... I have no one to run to. No mama to cry to. No daddy to hold me. Just me and my pain. So, I keep rotating men. I keep it physical. Because disappointment doesn't cut as deep when there's no heart involved."

She finally met my eyes again.

"I'm sorry, Kross. But I don't have the space to be ruined again."

I reached out and grabbed her hand. Firm, but gentle. She didn't pull away.

"I hear you," I said, my voice low. "And I ain't here to save you from your pain. I don't want to fix you. But I need you to know—when I touch you, I'm not touching your body. I'm touching every piece of grief you never said out loud. Every little girl still waiting for a mother's kiss or a father's embrace."

She stared at me, still trying to hold it in.

"I was raised by a woman like you," I continued. "My mama. Soft-spoken but steel underneath. My daddy fucked up a lot, but she stayed... not because she was weak, but because she was strong enough to outgrow him right in his face—and still let him be her man. She didn't break. She rebuilt herself and dared him to come correct."

I leaned closer.

"When I look at you, Rivah, I see that same fire. But I don't want to control it. I want to witness it. Feed it. Match it."

Tears welled in her eyes but didn't fall.

"And maybe you ain't ready to believe in love again. Cool. I'll wait. But know this—I don't want your body more than I want your peace. I want your mornings, your sighs, your random stories about your students. I want your tired. Your angry. Your silence. I want every version of you."

I ran my thumb along her knuckles.

"So if you need to run, I'll understand. But if you stay? If you let me in?" I exhaled.

"I won't be perfect, Rivah. But I'll be present."

After I told her I'd be present, she just shook her head and whispered, "You don't get it, Kross."

"I want to," I said.

She looked at me, broken but fierce.

"Men break us. They break us with lies, with empty promises, with the way they touch us like we mean everything—only to treat us like nothing when their ego needs feeding somewhere else."

"And when we finally snap... when we stop being soft, when we stop praying over niggas and start playing them—we become the problem. The bitter one. The hoe. The hard-to-love one."

She took a deep breath, like the truth was trying to strangle her on the way out.

"I've been the one who begged a man not to leave. The one who swallowed her pride just to keep a connection alive that didn't even serve her. I've been cheated on and blamed. Abandoned and gaslit. I've looked in the mirror and couldn't recognize myself from how far I shrunk trying to fit into a man's idea of 'wifey material.'"

She laughed, but it wasn't funny.

"So yeah, now I'm cold. Now I rotate. Now I do what I want and fuck when I want and ghost when I'm bored. But nobody ever asks why."

Her voice cracked again.

"Men just call us hoes. Crazy. Difficult. But behind every hoe is a story. A pain. A moment she stopped waiting to be loved and decided to survive instead."

She looked away.

"You say you'll be present, Kross. But they all start off present. It's when shit gets real that men vanish. When a woman is too heavy to carry. Too much to deal with. Y'all don't know what it feels like to constantly patch up your soul with eyelashes and lipgloss and a smile that says, 'I'm fine.'"

I reached for her face. I needed her to see me when I said this.

"Rivah. Listen to me."

Her eyes locked on mine.

"You are not too much. You are everything."

She blinked, slowly.

"You are rage in poetry form. You are heartbreak repackaged as resilience. You are softness wrapped in spikes because life never gave you space to be unguarded."

I leaned in, forehead resting against hers.

"And I know men have failed you. Left scars in places kisses can't reach. But I am not them. I'm not here for just the climax. I'm here for the crash. The aftermath. The rebuild."

"You don't have to shrink. Or smile when you're aching. You don't have to dim down your fire for me to stay."

I kissed her cheek—soft, loving.

"I want the woman who's been called too hard, too loud, too sexual, too opinionated, too cold. Because that's the woman who's survived."

"You'll leave."

"I won't," I said instantly. "So, let me be the reason you believe someone could stay."

She collapsed into my chest—not out of weakness, but because someone finally saw her.

And I held her. Not to fix her. Not to claim her.

I realized she didn't need saving, just someone who wouldn't flinch at the ruins and still choose to stay.

14

Rivah

I laid stretched out in Kross's bed with nothing but his shirt on and the silk sheets bunched between my thighs. The pillows smelled like him—rich, clean, and a little bit sinful. He was somewhere down the hall in his office, talking sharp on a conference call. Something about a last-minute deal and projections being off.

I wasn't paying too much attention because my best friend was on FaceTime looking like she was two blinks away from punching the air.

"Rivah, I'm so over these people. My auntie said, 'You used to be such a pretty girl.' Like dating Dakota made me grow horns or some shit."

I sighed, propping my phone up on Kross's pillow. "I told you, old people think if you don't follow their blueprint, you're building a house in hell."

"It's just—my whole family acting like I'm doing drugs in church. And Dakota already feels like she's not enough."

I sat up, tucking my knees under me. "Look, I ain't gon' lie; I didn't understand it at first, either. But you know what? It's not for me to understand. And it sure as hell ain't for them to approve."

"If that strap and that woman got you smiling in the morning, if she's loving you right, seeing you, choosing you every day—do that shit. Loudly. Unapologetically."

"I just don't want them thinking I'm turning my back on God."

I scoffed. "Vane... baby. Tell them you go before God alone. Not with your mama, your judgmental auntie, or your grandma who still got beef with Mother Jackson for wearing red to church."

She burst out laughing, hand covering her mouth.

"You so stupid."

"But I'm right."

"Yeah," she smiled, "you are. And Dakota... she really does make me happy."

"Then keep her. And keep a spare battery for the strap if you gotta."

That sent her over the edge, wheezing with laughter. I laughed with her until my phone vibrated again and I looked down at the screen.

Unknown Number.

My smile faded just a little.

"Who is it?" Vane asked, still catching her breath.

"Some unknown number," I said. "Lemme call you back."

"Alright. Call me back with tea, not trauma."

She hung up and I stared at the number, still ringing.

Then answered.

I pressed the speaker button, and I hadn't even said hello yet when a woman's voice slid through like she had a mission.

"Is this Rivah?"

I blinked. "That depends on who's asking."

She let out a light laugh like we were old friends catching up. "Harrison."

I repeated it back to her. "Harrison... Harrison... Harrison?" I paused. "Who the hell is Harrison?"

She didn't sound surprised. "Harrison is my soon-to-be fiancé."

I squinted. "Soon to be? Girl, who even says shit like that? Are you auditioning for Real Housewives or just delusional?"

"You may know him as number eleven."

And baby, when she said that, it clicked.

"Ohhhhhh," I laughed, damn near choking on air. "Harrison with the missing number 11 tooth and the 'I'm the prize' complex? My bad, sis. I forgot that man had a government name."

"Yeah. That one."

"Well, congrats... I guess? But what do you want with me?" I sat up in the bed, still grinning. "I haven't spoken to that man in a minute. So, you're good. I don't want him. Never did."

"I know you haven't," she snapped. "He wouldn't be that stupid to play with me. Plus, he's blocked, remember?"

I rolled my eyes. "Okay, and...?"

She inhaled sharply like she was about to drop some bomb. "I read that post that's been floating around on all those blogs. The viral one. And I know it's about him. The birthmark, the tooth... that's my man."

I could barely hold my laugh in.

"You mean the post that said he kept saying the woman was doing too much because she had rhythm and stamina he couldn't keep up with?" I chuckled. "Yeah, I read that. But again—what. Do. You. Want?"

"I'm calling to request that the post be deleted. Or else."

I raised an eyebrow and laid back on the pillow. "Or else what, ma'am?"

She cleared her throat. "Let's just say, it won't be pretty."

"Oh girl, please," I said, rolling my eyes so hard I almost saw Jesus. "You really calling another woman about a dick that was mediocre at best? Sis. You got it. I hope you and that repaired smile have a beautiful wedding. May the veneers stay tight."

"His smile's better than yours now."

"Well, duh, because he finally shut the fuck up. That's an upgrade in itself," I said with a grin. "You still ain't told me why you're really calling."

"I want it taken down. That blog post."

"And I don't know what you're talking about," I said sweetly. "You're making a lot of accusations for a woman calling another woman about a dick that clearly had to use Google Maps to find self-esteem."

"You're calling about a birthmark and a missing tooth like you're a private investigator for the Penis Protection Agency. Let me be very clear—if I knew the woman who ran that blog, I'd tell her to double post it just for the threat."

"You're disrespectful."

"And you're insecure. You're too worried about who had him last and not focused enough on why he left a paper trail that made it that easy to identify him. That's your problem."

"I'm going to get this handled." she threatened.

"Good luck, Nancy Drew. I hope when you find her, she beats your ass for wasting her time."

Click.

I tossed my phone on the bed, annoyed that a woman would even take the time out of her day to call me about a man who couldn't even keep up with a basic pelvic rhythm.

Before I could even exhale fully, I heard a deep laugh behind me.

I turned toward the bedroom door, and Kross was leaned against the doorframe.

"Number Eleven, huh?"

I squinted and grabbed a pillow. "How much of that did you hear?"

He pushed off the doorframe, walking toward me. "Oh, just about all of it. But I didn't want to interrupt before you started grilling my ass too. That whole birthmark and missing tooth combo had me invested."

"I don't even know why that woman called me about a man who ain't never been my problem. And what really pisses me off is that he gave her my number. Blocked means vanished, not forward my extension."

Kross sat on the edge of the bed, laughing so hard he nearly doubled over. "So let me get this straight... You really had the nerve to get some mediocre dick and head from a man with a missing tooth?"

I hit him with the pillow. "Shut up! I was young. Delusional. And he was cool over the phone. He did the whole 'facetime from the eyebrows up' thing. I didn't see the tooth till we were already past the point of return."

Kross laid back and pulled the sheets over his waist, still grinning. "Nah, Rivah. Ain't no way I can look at you the same after that. A missing main tooth? That's not even a red flag. That's a damn hazard sign."

I turned toward him and raised a brow. "Please. Don't act brand new like you haven't messed with hoes you look back at now like, 'what the entire hell was I thinking?'"

He raised a hand. "Guilty. I've had a few where I'd rather jump into traffic than admit I let them touch me."

"Exactly," I smirked. "So don't judge me, Judge Judy."

"Let me be real, I'm not judging. If you knew anything about Tubi, Foster Kid, or Cynthia, you'd clown me to hell and back."

I blinked. "Wait. What kind of names are those?"

Kross burst out laughing. "Man, it's a thing me and my brothers do. Been like that since we were kids."

I gasped, wide-eyed. "Please don't tell me y'all give people nicknames, too."

He nodded with pride. "Hell yeah. Can't help it. It's tradition at this point."

I snorted and threw my head back. "Wow. I feel so damn seen right now. I literally cannot talk to someone without giving them a nickname."

He smirked and leaned in. "Alright then, let me tell you how these legends got their names."

I adjusted myself against his chest, giddy as hell. "I'm listening."

He cleared his throat dramatically. "*Foster Kid*. That woman moved on so fast. Every man she dated, she'd move in within two weeks. Like she never had a key to her own spot."

I covered my mouth to stop my laugh.

"You could sneeze in her direction and she'd be looking for closet space."

"Deadass," he said, holding up his hand in oath. "Then there's *Tubi*. Honestly... the name speaks for itself."

I raised a brow. "Go on..."

"She was free entertainment. Did anything for attention. You could like her story and she'd send you a video. And I don't like easy pussy. That shit scares me. Why you tryna give it away so bad?"

I was wheezing. "Free streaming platform behavior."

"Exactly. Tubi behavior."

I was damn near rolling at this point, holding my stomach. "Okay, okay—what about Cynthia?"

That man could barely breathe from laughing. "So, my brothers pulled up to one of my rental condos while she was over there. She didn't know they were coming, and came out of the bathroom... without her wig."

He held back tears. "Her hairline looked like it had been scrubbed with an eraser. My brother was like, 'Bro, why does your girl look like Cynthia from Rugrats?'"

I choked. "NOOOOOO! Not Cynthia! Not Angelica's doll! You. Are. Going. To. Hell."

"Hell yeah," he said, still laughing. "But I swear I ain't know her shit was skint up like that. Had I known, I would've bought her a bonnet or something."

I buried my face in the pillow, laughing so hard I thought I might pass out.

Kross sat up and reached over to his nightstand. I thought he was grabbing the remote or something until I heard a jingle.

He turned and handed me a small black key fob.

"What's this?"

"My car keys."

I sat up straighter. "Your car keys... for?"

He leaned in, lips brushing my temple. "I gotta handle something. Business. It might take some time."

"You kicking me out?"

"Nah," he grinned, "I'm sending you home."

I tilted my head.

"Because tomorrow night," he said, eyes dark, "I'm taking you out. And after that, I'm bringing you back... and fucking the entire week out of you."

"I want you to go home," he continued, "do whatever maintenance you need to do. Wax, soak, stretch, meditate—I don't care what it is. Rest every part of that pretty ass body, Rivah. 'Cause I'm not showing it any mercy."

My thighs clenched just from the audacity of it all.

He leaned in and kissed me slow and deep, like he already had me bent over that damn bed again.

When he pulled back, he stood up and started slipping on his black tee and gold chain, looking too good to be legal.

He turned back toward me, lips curved in that sinful smirk. "I'll call you when I'm done, baby."

And just like that, he was gone.

Leaving me in his bed, heart racing, key in hand, and a countdown already ticking in my head.

15

Kross

I hadn't even been at my parent's house twenty minutes before Kendrix called, blowing up my line like his damn life depended on it. Three missed calls. Three frantic texts.

> **Kendrix:** Yo, I need you. Now. In person. No questions.

I didn't even respond. Just slid out the back door and told Ma I'd be right back. I called him while I headed to the location he sent me.

"Tell me this is about money or a body, and not some dumb shit," I said annoyed.

"It's worse."

"Who?"

He swallowed. "Remember that girl from back in February? The one with the green G-Wagon and the attitude problem?"

I nodded slowly. "The one Niv told you to stop fucking with."

"Yeah, her. She hacked into my phone, Kross."

I blinked. "What?"

"She figured out my damn passcode! I don't even know how. But she went through everything. And she got Niv's nudes."

Silence.

My jaw tensed. "Say that again."

"She got her nudes, man. Like—videos. Screenshots. Shit she would send me when I'm out and working."

I exhaled hard. "What does she want?"

"She hasn't said... yet. I'm about to pull up on her now. She sent the shit to my phone saying, *'Hope your spicy little secret's ready for the big screen.'*"

"Jesus." I gritted my teeth. "She post that shit and Niv gone catch a damn felony."

"You think I don't know that?" he shouted. "That's why I called you!"

I shook my head. "Give me 10 minutes and I'll be there."

I pulled up to the spot Kendrix sent, my dark tint from my windows doing little to dim the heat of what was about to unfold. I could already hear his voice before I even put the car in park.

"Man, you buggin' for real! This ain't even that deep," Kendrix barked, pacing in front of a petite, caramel-skinned woman in designer slides and a long ponytail. Her arms were crossed, phone in hand, and a smug look on her face.

"You're the one who made it deep when you let that bitch think she won," she said, her voice sweet with venom. "I don't care about that Niveah chick. I had you first."

Kendrix's jaw clenched. I knew that look. He was a breath away from snapping.

"Yo," I called, stepping out and slamming the door. Both their heads snapped to me. "Let's bring it down before somebody does something they'll regret."

The woman blinked as I approached, her smirk faltering just a little. I moved like I wasn't phased. That always made people nervous.

"You must be the other brother," she said, eyes raking over me like she was calculating something.

"And you must be the one dumb enough to play with a man's life like this," I replied evenly. "You hacked his shit. You threatening to leak private images. You do that and I promise you, it's not just Niveah you'll have to answer to."

She scoffed, "Please. What is she gonna do?"

Kendrix almost lunged but I put a firm hand to his chest.

"Stand down," I said, my voice low but with enough weight to make him still. "She's doing this to get a reaction, dumb ass."

I turned back to her. "What do you want?"

She tilted her head. "I want him to admit it. That I meant something. That Niveah isn't better than me."

I laughed. "You want validation, sweetheart? From someone who's already chosen? You really thought airing out somebody else's body would earn you closure?"

"She sent them to him, not you," I added. "You put those out and you're not just petty, you're criminal. Are you ready for that?"

She went silent.

"You got a lot of pain. I see it. But this ain't the move," I told her, softening my tone just slightly. "Delete the damn photos. Let it go and don't give us a reason to make this a bigger deal than it already is."

She rolled her eyes, but her finger hovered over the gallery. One by one, the photos disappeared.

Then, Kendrix—because his mouth has never known peace—muttered, "You lucky Niv ain't here. She would've fucked you up and posted that."

Her head snapped toward him. "Boy, fuck you. Niv don't scare me."

I stepped between them like a damn referee. "Both of y'all, shut the fuck up."

I turned to the girl, jaw clenched. "You might be a strong woman who can hold her own, but Niveah is not one to be fucked with. That woman will beat your ass on sight and then turn around and eat you alive in a courtroom."

I took a step closer, lowering my voice. "Because revenge porn ain't a slap on the wrist, sweetheart. It's jail time. You really wanna be fighting off a cellmate?"

She didn't say a word and I could tell her ego was louder than her logic.

"And look," I added, tilting my head toward Kendrix, "my brother? He's a dumbass. And just him asking me to be here should tell you he don't give a fuck about you."

Kendrix folded his arms. "I damn sure don't."

Her face twisted. "Could've fooled me the way you were blowing me up at 3 a.m., crying after that bitch dumped your ass."

He chuckled darkly. "That wasn't no cry, baby. That was nut withdrawal. Don't flatter yourself."

I put my hands up. "I don't give a fuck about all this back-and-forth. What I do care about is not turning on the TV and seeing your name under Obituaries because you tried to be slick and got murked behind some dick that never belonged to you."

She clicked her tongue, but she hit delete on the last photo and stepped back.

"Thank you," I said, flat but genuine.

She threw one last glare at Kendrix. "Fuck you and that hoe. Y'all perfect for each other."

She stormed back into her townhouse, slamming the door.

Kendrix ran a hand over his face. "Damn. Appreciate you, bro."

I stared at him for a long second. "Nah. Don't thank me. Listen—you playing with fire. You don't bring chaos to your woman's front door and expect peace when you get home."

"I ain't even fuck her, though," he said, voice low. "It was on some chill shit."

"There ain't no such thing as 'chill' when you have a girl, Kendrix," I snapped. "Your dumb ass probably fell asleep next to her and she went all through that phone. That's on you."

He nodded, rubbing his temple. "You right... I'm just... fucked up right now, man."

I slapped him on the shoulder. "Be smarter, bruh. 'Cause Niv probably already knows."

His eyes widened like a guilty little boy. "You think so?"

I smirked, walking toward my car. "I know so."

I pulled the door open, laughing as I slid in. "I'm gonna go call my woman. At least I'm not out here hoein' and dodging bullets like you."

16

Rivah

"You can do a nigga bad but I like to do em worst. Make him have to see a therapist or make him go to church, ay"

KenTheMan was thumping through my apartment like she paid rent there. Bass so heavy my neighbors could probably feel it in their kneecaps, but I didn't care. I was in my zone.

Standing in front of the mirror in nothing but my black lace thong and a bra that made my girls look like they had their own VIP section, I twisted my hips to the beat and watched my ass jiggle with every move smirking at my reflection.

"I still got it," I said out loud, grabbing the yellow sticky notes I kept posted around my mirror like my own brand of therapy.

I snatched the cap off a pen with my teeth and scribbled in thick, bold letters: **"YOU TOO MUCH WOMAN FOR THESE NIGGAS."**

I slapped it onto the mirror and blew a kiss at myself before bending over and twerking in slow motion—left cheek, right cheek. My own laugh echoed around the room because damn, I was a vibe.

Then my phone started buzzing across the bathroom counter.

"Alexa, cancel!" I yelled over the music, rolling my eyes as the beat cut off mid-bar. I grabbed the phone.

"Girl, what now?" I answered talking to Vane, still catching my breath from my performance.

"You sound like you on stage at Freaknik," Vane said, instantly making me snort.

"Close enough. I was pre-celebrating. Date night, remember?"

"Oh Lord," she sighed. "You about to let that man rearrange your kidneys again?"

"Absolutely," I said, slipping on my robe and grinning. "And I plan to look damn good while he does it."

I stood in my mirror blending my foundation like a bad bitch with bills paid and secrets kept. Vane was on speaker, but she sounded... off.

"I know you're doing your yearly hiatus or whatever—you're off Facebook and Instagram, being mysterious like a rapper's baby mama..."

I rolled my eyes. "Girl, what now? What happened?"

There was a pause on her end. Too long for my liking.

I froze with my brush mid-air. "Vane?"

"I just saw this post. His family posted a picture of him and said... he's gone."

My brow furrowed. "Gone where? To jail?"

"No, bitch. Gone gone."

I blinked. "Wait... who's gone?"

"666."

My hand slipped, dragging my eyeliner halfway to my damn temple. I gasped and slammed the pen down. "BITCH—WHAT?!"

"I swear to God, Rivah. I was just scrolling and his cousin posted a picture of him with a dove emoji, and the caption said, 'Rest easy, bro. We got your mama.' Like, what the hell?"

My whole chest locked up. "What do you mean *Rest Easy*? I just saw him on somebody's close friend's story in Houston with that big-ass iced-out chain on and a margarita!"

"That was last month! Rivah, they talking like he was un-alived."

"Are you SURE it's him? Like... 666?"

"Yes! They used his government name, but I recognized that face. I saw it enough with all those pictures you use to send of his ass."

"Girl, what the actual fuck is going on?" I whispered. "This is the third man that I've dealt with that's just... *poof*. First Conner, then Bracelet... and now 666?"

Vane's voice got low. "Rivah... this ain't funny no more. I think something's up."

I stared at my reflection, the sticky note behind me loud as hell now:

"YOU TOO MUCH WOMAN FOR THESE NIGGAS."

What if being too much... was getting them niggas erased?

I stared at my reflection again, and my heart was pounding like I was listening to trap.

"Did they say what happened?" I asked, trying to steady my voice and keep blending like my life wasn't shifting under my lashes.

"Nah," Vane said. "A few people in the comments saying they want justice, and if anyone has tips to contact the authorities. It's giving... suspicious."

I paused mid-swipe. "Damn."

I tried to play it cool. I tried to make it make sense in a normal way.

"He was flashy, though. Always posting money stacks and rentals. Probably just... the wrong crowd."

But my hand wouldn't stop shaking. My concealer brush hovered near my eye like it was scared to touch me.

"Damn," I whispered again. My stomach sank deeper than I let it show. But it was something about that one... it didn't feel like coincidence.

"Girl," I said, forcing a laugh, "you remember why I gave him the nickname 666?"

Vane laughed, "Yup. 6 figures. 6 feet. 6 inches. Classic Rivah."

"Exactly," I smirked. "That man had the height, but not the dick to match. But I don't know what type of demon stroke he was blessed with because those lil six inches worked pretty okay."

We both burst out laughing, but the heaviness was still there.

"And the crazy part is," I sighed, "a few months ago, I was on the blog talkin' bout how if I ever became a mom, it'd probably be by him."

Vane went quiet. I knew she remembered that post, too.

"He was successful, attentive, took care of his mama like it was a second job—which was cute... but not too cute, you feel me? The only problem was he wanted a damn Stepford wife. I'm not built for aprons and stay at home mom vibes, sis."

"Girl, right," Vane jumped in. "I'll never forget Turks. He was in the club poppin' bottles, but the second you wanted to go out.. Mr. Alpha Male turned into Mrs. Control Issues."

I laughed a little too loud, needing the sound to drown out the way my chest felt.

"Big bullshit energy," I said, shaking my head. "Always wanted me home while he made outside his whole damn residence nightly."

Then I added, darkly, "Guess now he is really home for good."

Vane exhaled. "Bitch..."

"I'm just saying," I shrugged. "I process through humor. You want me to cry about a man I haven't texted since Obama was in office?"

She laughed, but we both knew that weird feeling hadn't left either of us.

Then she got quiet. "You gonna tell Kross?"

I paused.

"Uh... probably not."

"Rivah," she said, with that big sister tone I hated and needed at the same time. "You need to. If y'all locked in like you say, if he's showing up for you the way you talk about, then you owe him that. He needs to know what's going on. What if this blog thing spirals? What if you need him to protect you?"

I waved it off with my free hand. "It's not that serious."

But the back of my neck itched with a warning I couldn't shake.

Before Vane could push more, my doorbell rang. I jumped slightly.

"Let me call you back," I said quickly.

"You good?" she asked.

"Yeah..." I lied. "I'm straight."

Before I even opened the door, I looked at my camera monitors.

Of course.

There his fine, impatient ass stood. One hand in his pocket, the other rubbing his beard like he was deep in thought. He had on all black, like he was there to collect my soul. I sucked my teeth.

"Why are you almost 45 minutes early?" I asked through the door.

He looked directly at the camera, smirking like he knew I was watching him even before I spoke.

"I missed you," he said, smooth and low. "Went this long not seeing you and it felt wrong."

I rolled my eyes, even though I blushed.

"That's real sweet and everything, but no. You get points for honesty, though."

I unlocked the door and pulled it open just enough for him to see me in my long satin robe—untied at the top just enough to show the lacy edge of my black bra. My hair was done, laid like I had a point to prove, but I still had one earring in and a makeup brush in my hand.

He blinked. Then blinked again.

"Damn," he said, scanning me from top to toe. "You not even ready and still out here lookin' fine as fuck."

I smirked, leaning against the doorframe.

"Keep talkin' like that and we might miss this reservation, sir."

He grinned and stepped in, already reaching for my waist, but I dodged him.

"Uh uh. Go sit your ass down and turn on the TV. You knew you were early. That's not my fault."

He held up both hands in surrender. "Aight, aight. Just a few minutes, right?"

"Twenty max," I said, already walking away.

I could feel his eyes on me as I walked back down the hallway, my robe sliding open a little more with each step. I didn't fix it, so I let him look.

I stood in my bathroom mirror, lining my lips with the same confidence I always painted on before I stepped into the world. My playlist had shifted to some sultry R&B, low in the background, and my focus was halfway on blending my concealer when I caught movement in my peripheral.

I turned slightly—then froze.

Kross was in my bedroom. Not just standing in the doorway, but walking... slowly. His fingers trailed along my bookshelf. His eyes scanned the framed photos on my dresser. His presence—big and calm—was soaking up every inch of the room I never let anyone step foot in.

"What are you doing?" I said, sharper than I meant to.

He looked over, hands down, eyes soft. "I was just—looking."

My heart raced. I walked toward him, brush still in hand. "Looking? You didn't ask. This is my space. You don't just walk into people's personal space like that, Kross."

He blinked, taken aback by the sudden shift. "Rivah—breathe. I wasn't tryna snoop. You've seen my space. Every inch of me—physically, emotionally. I just...I guess I wanted to see yours, too. The real you. Not the version you give the world."

I crossed my arms. "That doesn't mean you get to take it without permission."

A heavy silence settled between us. I could feel my chest rising, falling, too fast. Something about him being in there—in the part of me that stayed untouched, unbothered, unread—unraveled something deep I couldn't name.

Kross stepped closer but gave me space. He looked me in my eyes and said, gently, "Okay. Then tell me why. Help me understand why it rattled you so bad... 'cause I see it in your face. That wasn't just about a man walking in your room."

My jaw clenched. I wanted to deflect. Make a joke. Change the subject. But the way he stood there, present—not pushing, just waiting—it disarmed me in a way that scared me even more.

"My space..." I started, then sat down slowly. My voice dropped. He stayed quiet, just nodding.

"I've never lived with anyone. Never shared a bed longer than a night. When people are gone, when the world gets loud, this is where I go to just...be. And when someone walks in here without asking—it feels like my peace is being taken without my permission. Like they're claiming something that's mine when I haven't even offered it yet."

I blinked quickly, the sting behind my eyes catching me off guard.

"I don't get many safe spaces, Kross. I've had people leave me, break me, try to mold me. This room is the only place where I've never had to shrink or be strong. It's my reminder that I still belong to me."

His brow furrowed slightly, not in confusion—but in empathy. Real, rooted understanding.

He took a slow step forward.

"I hear you," he said softly. "I didn't mean to take that from you. I swear I didn't. I was just tryna find pieces of you to hold onto."

I looked up at him, my voice barely a whisper. "What if I don't know how to give them?"

"Then I'll wait," he said. "I'll wait 'til you're ready. But next time? I'll ask."

I didn't know what scared me more—how much I needed him to say that... or how much I believed he meant it.

"I'm sorry," I said, my voice soft but certain.

He lifted his eyes to mine.

"I didn't mean to snap like that. I just..." I exhaled, "I'm trying, Kross. I really am. This is new territory for me. Letting someone in. Letting someone close enough to shift the way I see things. You've done that, and I'm still trying to process it."

He moved slowly, sitting on the edge of my bed like he didn't want to disrupt the energy, just share it.

"I built myself to be this woman who doesn't flinch, doesn't fold, who keeps her heart in a chokehold because I needed to survive. I didn't think a man would come along and make me rethink so many things I said I'd never feel again. So I'm still figuring out how to let myself... soften. Without losing the power I fought so damn hard to gain."

Kross leaned forward, his elbows resting on his knees. "Rivah," he said, low and warm, "I don't want you to change. I love how loud you are. How free. How wild. You walk into a room like you own it because you *do*. I don't want to shrink that. Ever. I just want to exist next to it. Maybe catch it when it needs a break."

That made my eyes sting again, but I blinked fast.

"I just got a lot on my mind," I said. "Vane been on my ass, too. She's concerned about my safety."

"What do you mean—safety?"

"It's nothing," I started, but his face said don't play with me.

"No," he said firmly. "If it involves your safety, then it's my concern now."

I hesitated. "It's weird. But... a few of my exes... men I've dealt with. They've been dying, Kross. One after the other. Just... gone. Vane noticed it before I did. I mean, it's probably a coincidence. Right? But it still makes you think."

His whole posture changed. Still calm, but more alert.

He didn't speak immediately. He just nodded like he was collecting the information, placing it somewhere deep in that mind of his.

"I get why Vane feels like that. And I'm glad you told me. You should've. 'Cause now it's not just your problem." He stood and stepped closer, looking down at me. "You will be safe, Rivah. Not just because I care. But because my life depends on it. You hear me?"

I nodded slowly, feeling every word like it was armor being built around me.

He bent down, kissed me softly—one of those kisses that settles into your chest long after the lips leave—and then looked around the room, finally smirking.

"You really got sticky notes everywhere, huh?" he said, eyes landing on one above my headboard.

I smirked. "Affirmations. Reminders. Life rules."

He walked to one and read it out loud. "'Treat him like my son. belt to ass, he be trippin.'" He raised a brow. "Yeah... that tracks."

I shrugged. "You're lucky I ain't write something worse."

He laughed and smacked my ass playfully. "Finish getting dressed, psycho. We got dinner reservations. And after that, I'm tearing that body up again, so rest your legs while you can."

I laughed, walking toward my closet with a roll of my eyes.

"Alexa," I called, "play 'I Got Questions' by KenTheMan."

The music hit, and so did my grin.

I was walking into the world not just powerful... but protected.

17

Kross

She looked so damn good it didn't make sense. Black dress hugging every curve. Hair pinned just enough to show off her neck—one of my favorite places to kiss. She said she wanted to match me, but she didn't just match—she outshined.

The restaurant was intimate and sexy—dim lighting, jazz humming low from the corners, tables spaced far enough for privacy, close enough for curiosity. I reserved it for a reason. It was more than just dinner. It was confirmation.

When the server brought dessert out, Rivah leaned in with her usual smirk, but it quickly turned to confusion when she saw the plate:

Kross + Rivah written in chocolate across the white ceramic.

She looked at me like I just turned the world sideways. "What is this?" she asked, soft but unsure.

I took a breath, leaned forward, and didn't let go of her gaze. "I know you. I know you're not the type that wants to be boxed in or claimed like property. And I don't want to disrespect that. But I also know what I want—and that's you. All of you. Not to own you. To walk beside you."

Her lips parted, and I could see her body stiffen slightly, so I kept going. Gently.

"I don't need to say 'be mine'—I just want us to be us. I want to be a part of your days, not just your nights. I've heard the stories, Rivah… about your mama, your daddy, the silence you've had to sit in alone. And I'm not here to replace them. But I damn sure don't want you walking through life like you ain't got nobody. You got me."

Tears formed in her eyes before she could stop them. She looked down like she was ashamed of the emotion, and I squeezed her hand tighter.

"I'll try," she whispered. "That's all I can promise. But you make it so easy to... trust. To step outside what I'm used to."

I kissed her knuckles slow, one by one, not caring who watched. "That's all I ask."

We both sat back in silence, soaking in the moment. Just before I picked up my glass again, a couple walked past our table—and I caught movement in the corner of my eye.

I turned slightly.

And my heart slowed for half a second.

I knew her.

The woman on that man's arm.

And from the way her eyes widened the second she noticed me, I knew she wasn't expecting to see me either.

Rivah noticed. Of course.

She leaned in, squinting her eyes the way she always does when she's about to say some shit that makes the entire room stop breathing.

"Don't make me slap the fuck outta you, Kross. We just started this shit, don't play with me."

I burst out laughing, holding my hands up like I was under arrest. "Nah, baby, I promise. It's not even like that. It's just someone from my past. I just... know how she is. We haven't talked in a while, and I don't have time for the drama or bullshit tonight."

She relaxed a little, that mischievous glint still in her eye. "There won't be any bullshit. But she can try it." Her voice was sweet, but the warning underneath it was clear as hell.

I grinned and shook my head. "You not gon' believe this, but... that's Cynthia."

She blinked. "Cynthia?"

"Yeah..." I said, laughing already.

She repeated it again, like the name was slowly jogging her memory. "Cynthia... wait—CYNTHIA?! The snatched-up scalp Cynthia?!"

I couldn't hold it in. "The very one."

She gasped, clutched her invisible pearls, and then leaned back. "Oh I gotta turn around and see now."

"Go ahead," I chuckled, nodding toward her. "Get your peek in."

She turned around quick—lowkey, but not lowkey enough. And then she whipped back around with her eyes wide as hell. "Kross."

"What?" I said, sipping my drink, still amused.

"That nigga she with? That's Number Eleven!"

I damn near choked on my drink.

We both turned around in sync like two nosey-ass aunties. Cynthia and Number Eleven caught us mid-stare. All four of us locked eyes for a second—and then me and Rivah just lost it. Laughter shook the table, and she spun back around, clutching her chest.

"God don't like ugly," she whispered, dabbing her tears from laughing so hard.

"And apparently, He got jokes," I muttered, still wheezing.

Just as we were trying to recover from the laughing, Cynthia looked, her long-ass lashes blinking like they were about to take flight.

"Problem?"

The word cut the air and the whole restaurant went silent. Even the forks paused mid-air.

I didn't even get a chance to process it before I saw Rivah's whole demeanor shift. That calm, chill laugh turned to war in her eyes. Her lips parted just enough for her jaw to tighten. I grabbed her hand before she stood up and flipped the damn table over.

"Baby." I said. A plea and a warning wrapped in one word.

She smiled... but not that sweet, giggly smile. It was the smile women make before they ruin your life and sleep like a baby afterward.

"I'm not gonna do anything. I promise," she said, still holding my gaze. "But she asked if I had a problem... and I do."

Shit.

"Because," she continued, "if she's the bitch that called my phone about a nigga I BEEN blocked... then we already got beef. And now, to top it off, I find out she used to fuck MY nigga?" She pointed at me without even looking at me, and I swear my chest got tight in the best way.

She called me her nigga.

I should've stayed serious, but I felt my damn face heat up like a schoolboy with a crush. I tried to straighten my face but hearing her claim me had me blushing like a simp.

"I'm just sayin', it's too many overlaps and way too many coincidences. And I ain't never liked recycling." She stood up slow, graceful, her hand releasing mine. "Excuse me," she said, sliding her chair back like a lady but moving like a storm.

"Oh nah," I said, rising up too. "You are not going over there by yourself. I'm coming."

Because I already knew Cynthia didn't want a conversation. She wanted a scene.

And Rivah was the scene.

We made our way over to the table, and Cynthia's man looked like he was about to slide under the table and disappear.

Rivah cocked her head, voice laced with fake sweetness. "That new tooth looks nice," she said, nodding at him. "Smile for me, just once."

He looked like he wanted to die right there.

Cynthia folded her arms. "You talk real big online. You lucky I didn't sue your ass."

Rivah blinked, slowly. "Sue me? Girl, you barely survived that lacefront glue. Your whole scalp out here begging for help, and you worried about a post?"

The waitress two tables down gasped. Somebody mumbled "Oop—" under their breath.

Cynthia snapped, "That blog post was defamation. That was my man you were talking about. His birthmark, his missing tooth—"

"And?" Rivah cut her off. "You mad because the post was accurate? Maybe next time tell your man to keep his two inches, missing tooth, and broken ego away from real women."

Cynthia stood up. I stepped up, too. I wasn't going to let it get that far.

Rivah held out a hand to stop me, wanting all the smoke herself.

"You think you're the first bitter bitch mad about me rating her man?" she laughed. "I'm not the problem, sweetie. Your man is. If you are reading blog posts looking for his dick, maybe you should've written the review first."

"Don't talk to me like you know me," Cynthia snapped.

"I don't have to know you," Rivah replied, smiling wide. "But I do know your scalp is crying for mercy. Good luck, though."

Cynthia's man cleared his throat like he was about to speak, but Rivah threw a hand up. "Don't. Don't even try. You already gave your dick to the internet once. Ain't nothing you say from that seat gon' raise your rating."

I was fighting a laugh so hard it hurt. But it was the pride swelling in my chest that almost took me out. Rivah was wild.

"You called my phone over a penis review," Rivah added, louder now. "And had the nerve to try to check me over a nigga who couldn't keep up in missionary. You should be embarrassed."

Cynthia's lips were tight. She didn't expect the same energy back. Not with a man beside her and a crowd watching.

"Next time you think about calling me," Rivah said, stepping closer, "you better go home, oil your scalp, and moisturize your pride."

The room went silent.

Cynthia opened her mouth—then closed it. Her man just stared at the salt shaker.

I grabbed Rivah's hand and kissed it right there. "Let's go, baby."

As we walked back to our table, I heard someone at another table whisper, "She read the hell outta her." Another woman clapped. One man said, "Damn, that's his girl?"

Yes. Yes she is.

NETRAANTIONETTE

Back at the house, Rivah was posted up at my in-home bar like she owned the place—legs crossed, drink in hand, laughing like she hadn't just verbally demolished a bitch in front of a five-star restaurant crowd. I poured us both a double shot of Don Julio 1942 and slid her glass across the marble like I'd done it a thousand times.

"You know," I said, leaning on my elbow, "you really got a gift for making scenes look like art."

She lifted her glass. "Cheers to petty being poetic."

We clinked glasses.

The liquor hit warm, and I let the silence breathe for a second before asking the question that'd been sitting in the back of my head ever since Cynthia opened her cracked lips.

"So... that blog she mentioned. What's that about?"

Rivah gave me this dismissive little smirk, like I asked her if she recycled. "It's nothing."

I raised an eyebrow and took another slow sip, eyes never leaving her. "Rivah."

That's all I had to say. She sighed, rolled her eyes like I was annoying her, but the tension in her shoulders gave her away. She sat up straighter, tapping her nails against the glass.

"Alright," she said, "fine. A few years ago, I started this anonymous blog. I was going through some shit, and it started as me just talking crazy to Vane about these men I was dealing with. She thought it was funny. Told me I needed to put it online."

I blinked, slowly. "So you...reviewed them?"

She nodded, biting her lip, trying not to laugh. "Yep. I rate the sex. The lies. The red flags. I call out patterns. But unfortunately, I never say names."

I tilted my head. "You giving reviews to dick?"

"Basically," she said, cracking up. "But tasteful. Poetic. Sometimes petty, but always true."

I leaned back, cracking up, letting the drink warm my chest.

"Who knows it's you?"

"Just Vane," she said, locking eyes with me. "And now... you."

I nodded, letting that settle in. A part of me respected it. She took her pain and flipped it into power. A narrative. A platform. A movement, probably. But then the darker side started connecting.

"And the exes," I said slowly. "The ones who were unalived..."

Her face changed, but she nodded. "Yeah."

I sat the glass down, leaned forward, and stared at her for a long beat.

"So, that's why Vane was worried about you?"

She looked at me. "Yes."

She looked down into her glass. "I never meant for it to be serious. I didn't expect it to grow the way it did. But now it's too deep. And I can't delete it. The people... they expect it. Shit, they live by it."

I looked at her, studied the woman behind the blog. The girl who turned her pain into paragraphs. Who put her trauma on display and wrapped it in humor so the world wouldn't see her bleeding.

And damn if it didn't make me want her more.

I leaned in, resting a hand on her thigh.

I rubbed her knee and whispered, "You're safe with me, Rivah. Just don't rate me wrong or I'll show you to stop playing with me."

I picked my glass back up, tapped hers again.

"To the blog," I smirked.

She shook her head. "To surviving it."

She was quiet again, swirling the last bit of liquor in her glass before looking up at me with a smirk tugging at her lips. But there was something underneath it too. Like a weight.

"It's crazy that I've told you so much," she said, almost like she was confessing to herself. "I always said no man would get that kind of access to me again."

I leaned back, watching the way the candlelight danced across her face. "Some walls weren't meant to be broken. Some were just waiting for the right hands to help you climb out."

Her eyes flickered, and she grinned. "That was poetic. Cute."

She leaned toward me a bit, eyes narrowing like she was interrogating me, but playful. "Okay, Mr. Poet. Now that I'm telling you all my business—what about yours? Is there a possible baby somewhere? Crazy ex I need to beat up? Do you have a fake Instagram? OnlyFans? Any deep dark secrets I need to know about before I let you kiss me again?"

I laughed, then shook my head. "No secret baby. No crazy ex worth worrying about. I don't even like social media. I've had one serious relationship, though."

Her brow lifted.

"She was from a real conservative family. And she couldn't mesh with my world. Couldn't handle my brothers, our chaos, the unfiltered shit. Even though I loved her..." I sighed. "She made me feel like the best parts of me, the parts I grew up loving, were wrong. And that shit cut deep."

Rivah nodded slowly, and her whole body language softened. She knew what that felt like.

"So I closed my life off," I admitted. "Thought it'd be easier to keep women out of the real parts of me. The messy shit. The loud dinners, the family chaos, the unfiltered conversations. I like to joke, I'm unhinged, blunt, a little wild. But I'm human and realistic, too. And most women either want to fix it, tame it, or run."

She stared at me, eyes lingering longer than usual. "But you let me in."

"I didn't mean to," I said, smiling a little. "You just walked in like you owned the place."

She laughed, and the sound melted every sharp edge in the room.

I reached for her hand, brushing my thumb across her knuckles.

"You're different," I said. "And I see you, Rivah. For everything that you are."

She tilted her head. "Even the parts that are cold, or broken?"

"Especially those."

The way she looked at me made my chest ache. There was no defense in her eyes now. Then she leaned forward and kissed me.

It wasn't soft. It was deep, like her lips were telling me things her voice couldn't say yet.

I gripped the side of her face and kissed her back harder, pulling her into my lap. She straddled me, her hands slipping into my shirt like she was trying to get to my soul.

Our mouths moved in sync, and it felt like something was finally unraveling. Something honest. Unfiltered. I could feel her heartbeat pounding against mine through her chest.

My lips left hers and trailed down her neck, the slope of her collarbone, until she let out a moan that nearly made me lose all sense of patience.

"Say the word," I whispered.

She leaned down, her lips brushing my ear.

She said, "Take me to your room," and I swear, everything inside of me shifted.

Not just my dick. My whole fucking soul.

I stood with her still in my lap, holding her ass tight in my grip as I walked us to the bedroom. Her mouth didn't leave my neck, her teeth grazing just enough to make me curse under my breath. I kicked the door shut behind us, and dropped her on the bed like she was made to be there.

She leaned back on her elbows, watching me. The black dress she had on slid up just enough to drive me wild, showing that she had no panties on.

"You did this on purpose," I said, kneeling on the bed.

"I came ready," she smirked.

I didn't waste time. I reached under her knees, pulling her down to the edge of the bed. She gasped, and I smiled. Her lips parted again to speak but all I wanted to hear was her breath catch, and I got it as soon as my tongue hit her.

She moaned, loud and sweet, gripping the sheets and rocking her hips against my face. I took my time. I gave her every bit of control until I wanted it back.

I rose up and kissed her. Then I undressed. I watched her eyes drop to my dick and widen.

"You gonna sit there and stare?" I asked.

She smiled. "I'm memorizing."

She pulled the dress over her head, and I stood there for a moment—just *looking*. She was art. She was poetry I wanted to rewrite with my hands every night.

"You're beautiful, Rivah."

"Stop," she whispered. "You're making me feel things."

"Good." I climbed on top of her. "Now feel this."

When I slid into her, she cursed under her breath like she was losing her religion. Her nails clawed into my back, pulling me deeper, and I gave her all of it. All the emotion. All the pressure. Every slow stroke felt like I was digging into a part of her that no man had touched.

I wanted her scars. Her fears. Her pain. And I wanted her to feel safe giving it to me.

"Look at me," I whispered against her mouth. "I got you."

My hands gripped her ass, her waist, her throat. I sat up with her in my lap and whispered, "I want you."

And she whispered back, "Then take me."

I laid her on her back again and gave her the kind of stroke that made her scream into my neck. I could feel her pulsing, her body trembling under mine as I lost myself in her.

When I came, it was deep and raw and possessive.

But, I wasn't done.

18

Rivah

The weeks just continued to fly by and somehow, I went from rating men like Uber rides to falling asleep on FaceTime like a simp-ass teenager with Kross.

If we weren't tangled in his sheets finishing off a nightcap, we were whispering about nothing until one of us started snoring mid-conversation. He swore it was always me first. I swore it was him. We'd never agree, but the truth was, we were both just sprung.

And it was cute. Sickening, but cute.

I caught myself smiling in the middle of class and one of my students asked if I was texting "my sneaky link." I almost threw my Expo marker. Third graders had no business knowing terms like that.

We were in the middle of a very heated class debate about which body system was more important—nervous or digestive. It was hilarious how passionate my kids were.

"Miss Banks, I'm just saying... you could go a whole day without thinking hard, but you cannot go a day without eating," Jaylin argued, folding his arms.

"And you can't eat without your brain telling your mouth to chew," Kennedy snapped back.

"She ate you up," another student whispered behind his hand, and the whole class erupted.

I grinned, holding back a laugh. "Y'all are wild. Let's bring it down before someone says something about butts or poop—"

A knock came at the door, and I turned to see Principal Dale standing with an unreadable expression.

"Miss Banks? Can I see you in my office for a second?"

Immediately, the room ooooh'd like I was about to get suspended, arrested, and sentenced to twenty years all in one breath.

"Y'all chill," I said, grabbing my phone from the desk and forcing a tight smile. "I'll be right back. No chaos while I'm gone."

The walk from my classroom to Principal Dale's office felt like it stretched for miles.

I hadn't done anything wrong. Well, nothing fireable.

He gestured for me to come in, his usual forced-smile nowhere in sight. I stepped in, and he closed the door behind me, motioning toward the seat across from his desk.

A crisp manila folder sat in front of him, like some kind of silent threat.

"We've been receiving a few emails and complaints about you," he said, folding his hands.

"Really?" I raised a brow. "That's surprising because no parents have reached out to me."

"It's not related to the students directly," he said slowly. "Or classroom behavior."

I tilted my head. "Okay... so why am I here, exactly?"

He sighed like the conversation made him uncomfortable. Maybe it should've. He opened the folder and slid a few printed screenshots across the desk toward me. I stared down at the pages.

Blog post titles. Social media comments. Circles around certain lines.

"Are you familiar with a blog by the name of *Body Count*?" he asked carefully.

I blinked, confused. "No."

He looked unconvinced. "Well, this blog... it's been brought to our attention by a concerned individual. Apparently, it features posts that detail... explicit experiences, often rating men and using very detailed descriptions. There's a lot of speculation circulating that you are the anonymous author."

I paused. Let out a low laugh. "So, let me get this straight. You're sitting here, showing me some screenshots and rumors of a blog that could belong to anyone, and instead of asking me privately or investigating thoroughly, you're assuming I'm behind it?"

His face went pale.

"Miss Banks, I just—"

"No, let's be clear." I cut him off. "This is borderline defamation of character. You're bringing me in here, accusing me, a licensed educator, of running a sex blog based on anonymous tips? You didn't even do the bare minimum to confirm it?"

He cleared his throat and started fumbling with his pen. "It wasn't my intention to accuse. A woman called and said she was certain it was you. I should've... I should've handled it better."

I narrowed my eyes. "What woman?"

"I didn't get her full name. She just said you had been 'disrespectfully discussing her fiancé in detail.'"

I leaned back in the chair and let out a dry, bitter laugh. "Wow."

He started shifting again, realizing just how stupid he sounded.

"I truly apologize, Miss Banks. I—uh—I realize now this should have been handled more... delicately."

I stood up and smoothed my skirt. "No, you should've had some damn sense. If I had a dollar for every woman mad about a man that didn't belong to them, I could retire early. Next time, before you drag a Black woman into your office with allegations based on jealousy and gossip, maybe you should remember your own policy on professionalism."

He nodded furiously. "Understood. Completely."

"Good," I said, snatching the folder off the desk. "Because if I wanted to lawyer up, this whole hallway would be empty by Monday."

I turned to walk out, heels clicking again.

Then I walked right back to my classroom with my head held high.

NETRA ANTIONETTE

I was so annoyed, I could barely spell "photosynthesis."

Cynthia and her bald-headed-ass nerve really had the audacity to bring her mess into my place of employment? The same woman who called my phone about a man I didn't even want, got the nerve to start confusion where I get my direct deposit?

I was livid. Not the kind of mad that makes you scream, but the kind that has you sitting still... blinking slow... heart pounding.

I tried to stand in front of my class and give my usual lively science lesson. I really did. I stood there with the dry-erase marker in hand, looking at the board, my mind screaming *'fuck that bitch'* on repeat.

Finally, I sighed. "Alright y'all... laptop time."

Cheers exploded around the room like they were sick of me anyway.

"Get on the science games," I added. "Only the ones I said are okay."

They didn't care. Their lil fingers were already flying across keyboards, loading up simulations and quizzes with cartoon explosions and weird sound effects. They were in heaven.

Meanwhile, I was in hell.

I kept pacing. Sitting. Standing again. Tapping my fingers. Cracking my knuckles. I *wanted* to talk about it, but Vane was gonna give me that, *"I told you that blog post would come back to bite you in the ass"* speech. I wasn't ready for her judgment. I needed comfort. I needed calm.

I needed...

Ugh. Him.

I crossed my arms and stared at my phone screen like it was taunting me. I had told myself I wasn't gonna be that girl. But there I was, itching to call that man like he was an emotional support number.

I rolled my eyes and whispered to myself, "Girl, just call him."

I glanced up at my kids still engaged. Perfect.

I walked toward the back of the room where my desk sat like a throne behind a small divider wall. As soon as I was tucked away, I pulled out my phone and hit his name.

It rang twice.

"Hey, baby," Kross's voice came through, smooth like he already knew I needed it. "Everything alright?"

I closed my eyes, exhaling just from hearing his voice. "No. Not really. I just—"

I paused, blinking fast to stop myself from being dramatic.

He could hear it, though. The shift. The way my voice dropped.

"What happened?" he asked, more serious now. "Are you safe?"

I nodded even though he couldn't see it. "Yeah, I'm safe. Just irritated as hell. I'll tell you, but I needed to hear you first."

"You got me," he said, his tone calm but full of quiet strength. "I'm listening. Take your time."

As soon as I heard that, I let the words pour.

"They pulled me into the office," I said, keeping my voice low so my kids wouldn't hear. "The principal had a damn folder in front of him like I was being investigated by the FBI or something."

"What the fuck?" Kross yelled on the other end. "For what?"

"They've been getting emails," I sighed, shaking my head. "Complaints. Talking about a blog named *Body Count*... asking if I'm the one behind it."

He went silent. That kind of dangerous quiet that made my spine straighten. "Baby... what?"

"Yeah," I huffed. "Some anonymous ass email talking about the blog is 'inappropriate' and against school policies. Accusing me. And of course, instead of investigating like a professional, the principal just slid the screenshots across the desk like it was proof."

Kross let out a slow, heavy breath. "Cynthia. That bald-headed, bitter-ass—"

"Mhmm," I cut in.

"She really brought this shit to your job?" he asked, his voice rising. "See, now I'm fucking mad."

"You think I'm not?" I whispered, clutching my desk. "I'm fuming. I don't even know how I'm keeping it together."

"But, how the fuck she even know where you work?"

I paused for a beat, then said honestly, "Because one thing about me—I never lied about my name. And if she got even a hint of who I was, and she's as jealous and obsessive as I think, it wouldn't take her long to Google, reverse-search, and start putting shit together. Especially with how wrapped around my finger you are."

He let out a low laugh, but it was tight with anger. "Yeah I let you think that, but nah she went too far with this."

"She's pressed," I said. "But dragging it to my place of work?"

"Is fucked up," he muttered, voice deadly calm. "Let me handle it."

I paused. "Kross..."

"I'm serious. I know you can handle your shit, but this ain't about just you anymore. This reached your job. So, now I'm asking... Can I handle it?"

I looked around, made sure the kids were still locked in on their games, then whispered, "Are you gonna tell me how you plan on handling it?"

"Of course," he said. "You'll know everything. But just know... I don't play when it comes to you. And I damn sure won't let anyone play with you."

My lips lifted into a slow smirk, even as heat rose in my chest. "You up to something."

"You know I am."

"And I cannot wait to see it."

His voice softened. "Calm down, baby. Finish your day. Be the badass teacher they love so much. I'll see you later."

That deep tone of his made the tension in my chest loosen just a little.

"You made me feel better," I murmured.

"I always will."

I smiled, then whispered, "I'll call you later."

"You better."

I hung up and leaned back in my chair, trying not to grin like an idiot while chaos brewed all around me.

Whatever Kross was planning....

I hoped Cynthia had her wig ready and glued down... because it was about to be snatched.

19

Kross

My blood had been boiling since Rivah called. Play on Instagram all you want. Get messy in the comments. Hell, even lie in a group chat. But going to my woman's job? Putting her career on the line? That was suicide wearing lip gloss.

I tossed my phone on the marble counter and cracked my neck. For a second, I let myself breathe. Not because I was calming down, but because I needed to focus. Women like Cynthia didn't respond to rage. They fed off it. Nah. I had to be surgical.

I picked up my phone again and opened our old thread.

Messages.

Back to back.

Ignored.

Month after month. Her talking to herself. Double, triple texting. Apologizing. Flipping the tone when I didn't respond. Gaslighting her own damn imagination.

I scrolled until I couldn't anymore. I hated seeing her name.

But I tapped call.

And just like I expected…She answered on the second ring.

"Kross?" she breathed like the phone was her lifeline.

"Yeah," I said calmly, rubbing my jaw. "It's me."

"Well damn," she chuckled. "It's good to hear from you. Took long enough."

I let out a short laugh, cold and hollow. "It's been a while, yeah. But I think we both know why I'm calling."

Silence.

Then she cleared her throat. "I figured," she said. "I'm not about to let anyone disrespect me, though."

I smirked. "You feel disrespected... by something you started?" I asked, tone sharp enough to slice concrete. "Make it make sense."

She sucked her teeth. "What pissed me off more is finding out it's her. That she's who you're with."

There it was.

The root.

The rot.

I had her right where I wanted her now.

"Look," I said, changing tones. Smooth. "Let's sit down. Talk this out like adults. You've clearly moved on. I have, too. We don't need to drag this any further."

She perked up. "I agree. I've moved on. I'm not technically committed but... yeah. I've healed."

"Good," I nodded. "Drop the location. I'll slide through. Let's talk."

"I'm home alone for a few hours," she said lightly. "Just text me when you're outside."

"Bet."

I ended the call and immediately opened my recent calls.

Tapped **Kendrix**.

He answered on the first ring.

"Yeah, bruh. You ready?"

"I'm ready," I said, grabbing my keys. "And bring Niv with you."

NETRA ANTIONETTE

I pulled up Cynthia's address and parked down the street instead of right in front. The thing about women like her—they live for a show, and I wasn't giving her one unless it was on my terms.

Niv hopped out of Kendrix's passenger side with her shades on and a Starbucks cup like this was just another day.

"You sure you want me doing this?" she asked, smirking as she adjusted her crop top and slid out a glossy lip balm.

"I brought you for a reason," I said. "And it ain't to babysit."

She sipped her drink. "Then let's make this quick. I still got a massage at 4."

We walked up together. Cynthia opened the door with her robe tied like she was trying to do everything but talk. Her face shifted when she saw Niv standing next to me, but before she could say a word, Niv brushed past her like she lived there.

"Cute robe," Niv said. "You bought it or did you keep it after somebody nutted on it?"

Cynthia's mouth dropped. "Excuse me?"

"No, I'm not excusing shit," Niv said, dropping her purse on the couch and kicking off her heels. "What you won't do is fuck with my girl's job 'cause you mad she got the man you couldn't keep."

I stood back and crossed my arms. This was exactly why I brought her.

Cynthia looked at me like I was gonna save her. I didn't blink.

"You came to my house to threaten me?" Cynthia snapped.

"No," Niv said, walking slowly toward her, "I came to enlighten you. Threatening would be me slapping that synthetic lace off your scalp and stuffing it in your throat."

Cynthia took a step back. "This is harassment."

"Oh baby, you ain't seen harassment yet. But let's be clear—if you ever contact Rivah's job again, if you ever speak her name, if I so much as hear you breathe wrong in her direction... I'll make sure your next job application gets redirected to hell. You wanna play petty? I'm professional at it."

"She wrote about my man!"

"Your man who gave her the dick, and had the audacity to do it with a birthmark and a missing tooth. You should be writing him up, too."

Cynthia's eyes welled, and Niv tilted her head. "Oh, don't cry now. You were bold when you called the school, right? Where is that energy at?"

Cynthia looked at me again. "Kross, are you really gonna let her—"

"I brought her," I cut in. "You poked the wrong bear, sweetheart. Rivah is mine. So if you come for her again, I promise I'll let Niv off the leash."

Cynthia smirked like she thought we were bluffing. "Y'all must think I'm scared of some stripper-looking hoe with a loud mouth."

I exhaled.

Niv turned around slow, like she was giving her one last shot at life. "Now girl, I done gave you your out. Don't let the looks fool you, because I'll drag you so bad your ancestors will feel it."

Cynthia scoffed. "All that talk and still ain't swung. You and that bitch y'all keep trying to protect must be scared of—"

SMACK.

That was it.

Niv's palm cracked across Cynthia's face so hard the robe slipped off one shoulder and her whole body turned like her spirit got yanked.

Before she could even recover, Niv grabbed her by the back of her neck and started going to work—slapping, snatching, hitting her so hard and so fast it sounded like applause.

I blinked. "Oh, shit."

Cynthia was yelling, "Wait! Wait!" but it was too late. Niv had locked in.

"I told you! I told you!" she shouted, snatching Cynthia's wig halfway off.

I saw Cynthia try to crawl and Niv pulled her back like a toddler that disobeyed in Target. "Get your ass back here! You wanted to talk shit, right? Talk now!"

I took two steps forward to try and stop it, but paused.

I love my face. I wasn't about to lose a tooth over a fight I knew better than to get in between. That's Niv's department. So instead, I pulled my phone out and called my brother.

Kendrix answered on the second ring, sounding like he was in the car smoking a big blunt "Yeah, bruh?"

"Come get your girl."

"Man, what is she doing now?"

"She beatin' the brakes off Cynthia. I'm talkin' full-blown Mortal Kombat, bruh. She might kill her if you don't come soon."

He laughed. "Damn. Already?"

"She called Rivah a bitch and said she wasn't scared. Niv snapped."

"I'm coming."

A minute later, Kendrix came flying through the door, hoodie on, chains swinging. "NIV! C'mon, girl! Damn!"

She was still yanking Cynthia's hair like it owed her money. "Let me go! Let me go! She said she wasn't scared, right? Lemme finish!"

Kendrix scooped her off the floor like a toddler mid-tantrum. "Baby, you made your point. You won. She's BLEEDING, shit!"

Niv huffed, still trying to reach over his shoulder like she had one more combo move to hit. "Don't ever in your life bring her name up again, bitch!"

I looked down at Cynthia. Wig gone. Robe twisted. Lip bleeding. Eye swelling.

Pitiful.

"Niv gave her the premium ass-whooping," I muttered under my breath.

Kendrix hauled her out the front door, still yelling. I followed him, shutting the door behind us.

I felt a little bad for Cynthia.

But she was warned.

Twice.

NETRA ANTIONETTE

Rivah was already stretched out across my couch when I got back to the house like I told her to be, one of my hoodies swallowing her up, legs tucked under her and that fire-ass smirk on her face.

"Okay," she said, as soon as I walked in, "don't make me wait. Tell me everything."

I tossed my keys on the counter, grabbed a water from the fridge and leaned against the island like I was about to deliver a sermon. "First off," I started, "Niv? That woman is not from Earth."

Rivah's eyes lit up, and she leaned forward. "Stop playin' and tell me what happened!"

I grinned. "Cynthia ran her mouth... Niv rearranged her dental plan. Simple."

Rivah damn near slid off the couch laughing. "You lyin'! Like... she really hit her?"

"Nah," I said with a straight face. "She beat her ass, Rivah. I ain't never seen a grown woman scream 'wait!' and crawl like that."

She was howling, face red, hand over her mouth. "Oh my God. I'm so mad I missed it!"

"She snatched her wig off and tossed it on the table like it was a damn centerpiece. Kendrix had to run in and carry her out like she was being evicted."

"Man, damn!" Rivah wheezed, still trying to catch her breath. "That's some shit you have drinks over. I need to take Niv out immediately."

I walked over, sat next to her and brushed her hair behind her ear. She was still giggling, but her smile slowly softened.

"I wish I could've done it myself," she muttered, "but... I'm glad somebody did. Ain't nobody ever showed up like that for me before."

Her voice dipped right at the end. That familiar shift. The vulnerability creeping in behind the walls she always kept up.

I watched her for a second, then pulled her into me, pressing my lips to her forehead. "You don't have to handle everything alone any more. I got you, Rivah. All of you."

She let her head rest on my chest, and I could feel her exhale like she was finally releasing something she'd been holding for years.

"I'm not used to this," she whispered. "Having someone see me for real. Not just the body or the mouth or the vibe. But like... me. And still show up."

"I see you," I said, pulling her in closer. "All the attitude, all the trauma, all the pretty... and I want it. I choose it. That's the difference."

I kissed her, soft and slow. She melted into it, and my hand slipped between her thighs.

But then my phone buzzed on the table behind me.

I groaned and leaned back to check it. Kendrix.

Yo. Slide outside. Need to holler at you real quick.

I kissed Rivah one more time before standing up.

"Go take a shower," I said, smirking. "Get comfortable. Be ready for me when I get back inside."

She raised an eyebrow. "Ready like..."

"Like ready," I repeated, licking my lips. "And leave the hoodie on. Or don't. Your call."

I winked, grabbed my phone, and walked out the door—already wondering what the hell kind of mess Kendrix had for me now.

20

Rivah

The hot water hit my back like a lover with patience, and Summer Walker hummed through the speaker like she was writing the soundtrack to my thoughts. I closed my eyes and let the steam fill the space, my hands moving slow over my skin like I was washing off everything that used to weigh me down. Ain't it wild how peace feels when you aren't used to it?

I let out a small laugh, barely realizing I was smiling to myself like a damn fool. "Girl... is this what the soft life feels like?" I whispered, tilting my head back under the stream.

Not even just the sex, but the safety. The presence. The feeling of not having to do it all by myself.

"Whew, girl," I muttered, cutting off the water and grabbing the towel. "You're in love, huh? Got you in here acting like them same thirsty hoes you judge on Facebook."

I laughed out loud at my reflection while drying off, cheeks glowing like I had a secret. I stood in front of his mirror, still dripping a little, towel clutched in one hand as I looked myself over.

"Stand tf up, Rivah," I told myself. "Get it together. You are weak in the knees, baby."

But then I paused, tilted my head, and whispered with a grin, "But he is a good man, Savannah..."

I giggled like a damn schoolgirl and nodded. "It's okay you fell, babe. That man was strong enough to make sure you ain't hit your face."

I hit my skin with some Nubian Nectar Oil from Bare Naked Essentials, humming to myself as I slid into a lace set that made me feel like a goddess and a problem all at once. Still no sign of Kross yet, so I tied on one of his robes and walked into the kitchen.

I poured a glass of wine, just enough to warm my chest and keep the mood going. I leaned against the counter, sipping, when I noticed the basement door. Cracked open just enough to tempt me.

Now, I'd seen every inch of his house. Hell, I'd been bent over most of it. But the basement was his spot. His creative lab. The place he went when he needed to engineer, think, breathe.

I always respected that space. Never touched it.

But... lately, he'd seen every part of me. Even the parts I used to hide. My blog room, my trauma, my joy. Everything.

"Just a little peek," I said to myself, swirling the wine in the glass. "Let me see what kinda nerd I'm really dealing with."

I smirked, robe clinging to my curves, wine in hand, and tiptoed toward the basement.

But curiosity? That bitch didn't come with a leash.

I pushed the door open slowly. The air shifted. It was colder. I stepped down the stairs, barefoot and hesitant, telling myself I'd only peek.

The moment I hit the bottom, my body stilled.

This wasn't a workshop.

There were no half-finished inventions, no wires tangled with screwdrivers or hardware.

There were screens. Computers. Desks. Wires everywhere. It looked like NASA met the CIA and had a tech-obsessed baby with too much money and time on their hands.

And then I saw a wall.

A fucking wall... of me.

Pictures. Dozens of them. Some I'd posted, some I hadn't. Some I didn't even remember taking.

But that wasn't the worst part.

Next to my pictures, there were others. Pictures of men. Familiar faces. Faces I knew. Men I'd written about. Screenshots from my blog posts. Printed. Highlighted. Annotated in red ink.

"No..." I whispered, stumbling back a step, wine sloshing out the glass. "What the fuck is this?"

A chill ran up my spine. My legs were ice. My heart was pounding so loud it was echoing in my ears. I moved like I wasn't even in my body anymore—floating toward a desk where a framed photo sat like a goddamn shrine. A picture of me and Kross. Taken just a few weeks back. Smiling like we had forever ahead of us.

My hand shook as I picked it up. A tear slipped down my cheek.

Then I heard him.

"Baby?"

I dropped the frame. The glass shattered against the floor like my last bit of peace. Panic flooded my veins.

His voice was closer. Urgent. Frantic.

"Rivah—baby, are you down there?"

I couldn't breathe. My lungs squeezed, my chest burning as I stared at the pieces on the floor, pieces of a moment that now felt like a fucking lie.

His footsteps pounded down the stairs.

I froze.

Trapped.

When he reached the bottom, his eyes locked on me—and I'd never seen him look like that. Not Kross. Not my Kross. His face was pale, jaw clenched so tight it looked painful, pupils blown wide like the world was caving in on him.

"Shit..." he whispered. "Baby, I can explain—"

"What the fuck is this, Kross?!" I screamed, stepping back, shaking so bad the robe belt slipped undone, hanging loose like my sanity.

He didn't move. Didn't blink.

"You—you have a wall of me?! Of men I've slept with?! You've been keeping tabs on my blog?!" My voice cracked, broken and laced with rage. "Were you planning something? Were you going to kill me? Is this some twisted shit?"

"No!" he shouted, voice raw. "Rivah, listen to me! That's not what this is!"

I laughed. A sick, hollow laugh. "Then what is it? Explain it to me, Kross. Explain why the fuck I'm standing in a surveillance room dedicated to my life like I'm some fucking obsession."

Silence.

I saw it in his face. The hurt. The fear.

But that didn't stop my heart from crumbling.

"Don't come any closer," I said, backing up until my back hit a table.

He took a slow step forward anyway.

"I wasn't tracking you to hurt you, Rivah," he said. "I was protecting you."

"From what?!" I screamed. "From the men I already stopped fucking? From myself? Or from the woman I was before you came and made me believe I could be loved and safe at the same damn time?!"

He winced.

"You don't understand." he said quietly.

"No. You don't understand what this looks like," I hissed, tears running down my face. "It looks like betrayal. Like control. Like I fell for a man who was already twenty steps ahead of me before I even gave him my number."

He moved closer, slowly, like I was a bird with a broken wing he was trying not to scare.

"I didn't lie to you, Rivah. I never lied. You told me you had a blog. You told me men were dying. You told me you felt unsafe. I figured it out, yeah. I read between the lines. But I didn't come for you to hurt you—I came for you because I needed to know who the hell was responsible for all this. I needed to know who was risking your life."

"And then what?" I said, voice breaking. "You kept the wall? You—framed the pictures? This isn't care, Kross. This is insanity."

He looked like I'd punched him in the chest.

But I was already gone.

Not physically. My feet didn't move.

But my heart?

It shattered on the floor, right next to that goddamn picture frame.

I couldn't move. My fingers curled around the wine glass like it was the only thing keeping me upright. My heart felt like it was about to crawl up my throat. This wasn't just a secret... this was a fucking movie script. Some Lifetime network on steroids type shit.

"I want the truth," I said, steady as I could despite the way my knees threatened to give out beneath me. "And you better tell me all of it. Because this—" I motioned to the damn horror story around me—"this shit didn't just start."

Kross exhaled hard. "Can we sit down and talk about it?"

"No," I snapped. "Talk now."

He looked at the floor between us. His jaw clenched. "Can I at least come closer?"

"Fuck no," I said, sharper this time. "Get to talking."

His brows pinched. "You're barefoot and there's glass on the floor. Just... Can you please move away from it?"

I walked straight over to his desk and sat my bare ass on it, legs crossed like a damn queen on her throne. "I'm good. Get. To. Fucking. Talking."

He swallowed. "I told you I was an engineer. That's true. I'm a software engineer. I just wasn't direct... because I didn't want to raise any question marks."

I stared at him.

"I got contacted months ago by a private client," he said slowly. "They wanted me to track down the creator of a blog. *Body Count.* At first, I thought it was just some catty, gossip site. But when I started digging, I realized it was... deeper. It was you."

My throat tightened.

"I did my job. Went through digital footprints. Metadata. Cross-referenced language patterns. Location tags. The deeper I dug, the more I found you. Your voice. Your pain. And yeah... your men."

I said nothing. Just waited.

He stepped slightly to the side, keeping his distance. "Rivah, I know it sounds fucked up. But I was supposed to find you and deliver everything I knew. Instead, I kept reading. I kept watching. I kept listening. And the more I did, the more I realized I couldn't hand you over."

My brows furrowed. "Why?"

He looked me dead in my face. "Because someone didn't just want to expose you, Rivah. They wanted to eliminate you."

The wine glass slipped from my fingers, shattering on the floor beside the broken frame. I flinched but didn't look away.

He nodded like he'd expected that. "You had a whole fan club. Not fans like groupies—fans like a cult of men who hated you. Men who thought you embarrassed them. Thought you made them look weak. And a few of them were powerful enough, angry enough, to start planning some shit."

My stomach twisted. "So... what? You killed them?"

"I neutralized the threats."

I choked on my breath. "What the fuck, Kross."

"They all weren't men you knew," he continued calmly. "Three of them were just internet egos with too much access. But two of them... yeah. You slept with them, and they acted like they didn't know you to hide their identity of being one of those men from their group."

I started crying, silent tears trailing down my cheeks.

"Bracelet?" I asked, barely above a whisper.

He nodded. "He was one of the worst. Initiated the group. Kept tabs on you and encouraged them to find you and hurt you."

"I didn't know—he was—he seemed..."

"Baby," he said, voice dropping low and deadly. "You can't fuck with felons who have nothing to lose. And with the kind of pussy you got?" He smirked, but it wasn't funny. "Niggas will kill for it. Or kill you over it."

My legs stiffened, but I didn't move. "What about 666?"

He sighed. "He was calculated and felt if he couldn't have you, no one else could, either. He knew you had a level of respect for him, especially after you wrote about him, maybe being a potential baby daddy if you wanted that. He secretly always wanted more, but you wouldn't change to his wants. He was just quieter about it, but just as dangerous. He needed to go."

I could barely breathe. "How many?"

"Five."

My heart stopped.

I stared at him like he was a ghost. "And... Connor?"

He smirked again. This time, it chilled me.

"That was personal."

"Personal?"

"He started all this. Broke you. Betrayed you. Built those walls around your heart like a fucking architect. He doesn't get to do that and walk away like nothing happened."

"You killed a man because he broke my heart?"

"I killed the man who turned you into a version of yourself that thought she wasn't worthy of real love."

A sob broke in my throat.

"You wouldn't have been on that blog writing about pain if it weren't for him. You wouldn't have needed walls if he hadn't demolished your foundation."

I stared at him, trembling.

"You think you're crazy, Rivah?" he asked, stepping just a little closer. "You're not. You're hurting. And I've spent the last few months loving every broken, brilliant piece of you. I didn't fall for your blog. I didn't fall for your looks. I fell for the way you survived. I just made sure the world wouldn't take you before you knew what it felt like to be safe."

I dropped my face into my hands and finally let it go. Let it all go.

Because I was terrified.

Because I was seen.

Because he'd killed for me.

And some sick, twisted part of me didn't feel afraid.

It felt protected.

And that scared me the most.

21
Kross

I stared at the wall. It did look like a fucking FBI murder board.

And she was just sitting there. Staring at me like I was a stranger.

"This is insane," she whispered, but it felt like it echoed off the walls. "You planned this. You inserted yourself into my life, played the long game, and fucked me with information you collected."

Her voice cracked at the end, and I felt something inside me fracture.

"How do I even know what was real... and what was just you doing your job?"

I opened my mouth, but couldn't find the words to say. Because what the fuck do you say to a woman who's right?

"It stopped being a job the moment I saw your face," I said finally, my voice low—honest.

"Rivah..." I softened my tone, that same tone I always used when I wanted her walls to drop.

She didn't wipe her tears or blink them away. She just let them fall.

"I trusted you," she said, her voice so small it could've shattered me.

"I protected you."

"By killing people?"

"They weren't people to me," I snapped. I hated the way that sounded, but it was the truth.

"They were threats. You think this was just about bruised egos? One of them had an entire thread about hiring someone to snatch you up. Said it'd be 'poetic justice,' and how you needed to be taught a lesson."

Her lips parted, but nothing came out.

I continued before I lost my nerve. "You think I was gonna sit on my hands and let that happen?"

She looked down at the shattered picture frame on the floor.

A photo I loved.

Her smile. Her light. That day she laughed so hard she spilled wine down her shirt.

That picture was cracked now. Just like us.

"And now what?" she asked quietly. "You think I'm supposed to go upstairs and cuddle with you? Like you didn't turn your love for me into a goddamn kill list?"

I exhaled hard. Stepped closer.

"No," I said. "I don't expect anything from you. I just want you to hear me."

"I did every over-the-line, dark, fucked-up thing I did because for the first time in my life, I found someone worth burning the rulebook for. Worth protecting without a second thought. You."

She was trembling.

Still barefoot. Still vulnerable.

And still not sure if she was standing across from her protector or her predator.

"You should've told me," she said.

"You would've run."

"You don't know that."

"I know you," I whispered. "Even before you knew me."

She closed her eyes, and I watched her shatter silently.

"You had no right to play God with my life," she said.

I moved closer, slow and careful. My hand hovered near her waist, not touching.

"I wasn't trying to play God." My voice cracked. "I was trying to save an angel who didn't even know her wings were on fire."

Her eyes flew open, wet and sharp.

"You don't get to call me that."

I took that hit and let it bruise my chest from the inside out.

"Then what do I call you?" I said, almost broken. "Because from the moment I saw you, I knew—there's only two ways this ends."

I stepped even closer.

"Either I die for you..."

Another step.

"Or I spend every damn day proving I was worthy enough to keep you breathing."

She hadn't moved. Not even a blink when I said it that I would die or live proving myself for her.

Her eyes glistened. Red. Wet. But her voice, when it came, was steady and sharp.

"You had every chance to tell me."

She didn't yell it. That's what hurt the most.

"I asked you," she said, her hand pressing into her chest like her heart was literally breaking. "I asked you if there was anything I needed to know. If there was something you were keeping from me. And you lied. You stood in front of me and chose to love me through lies."

"Rivah..."

"No." She cut me off. "We've had so many moments. Real moments. In that hotel room. On your couch. In your bed. On your damn barstools." Her voice cracked again. "I told you about my parents. My fear of being alone. My trauma. My pain. And the whole time, you were playing detective, judge, and executioner."

I ran a hand down my face, trying not to break.

"Because it wasn't easy to say."

"But it was easy to do?"

Her words hung in the air like smoke.

I swallowed hard. My chest throbbed as I looked at her—the woman who I would do anything for, even if it destroyed me.

"I planned to delete everything once I knew you were okay," I confessed. "Wipe the wall. Clear the files. Walk away like none of it happened. But every time I got close, I looked at you and couldn't. Not because of control." I shook my head. "Because I didn't want to forget a single part of how I found you."

She blinked slowly, and I saw the moment it hit her.

"You thought you were saving me," she whispered. "You thought you were the good guy."

"I wanted to be the one to make it stop. The pain. The fear. The shit you never said out loud but wrote like your life depended on it. I didn't want to change you, Rivah. I meant what I said. I love how wild and honest and powerful you are."

I stepped forward again.

"I just wanted you to feel safe enough to tap into your soft side. I know you've never had anyone to carry your load for you. No one to say rest. No one to say, 'I got it.'"

I breathed, voice thick with everything I was finally saying.

"I want a life with you. Not a fake, perfect one. A real one. With the hard shit and the healing. I want to wake up next to you. Learn your moods. Memorize the curves in your voice when you're pissed off or turned on. I want to meet your students. Help you grade papers while you bitch about kids who won't sit down."

She laughed then, barely, and I swear my heart cracked open at the sound.

"I want to build a life where you don't have to look over your shoulder. Where the only bodies we bury are our past selves."

That was when she started crying harder.

"I love you, Rivah."

She covered her mouth with one hand, like the words hit her somewhere she didn't want them to.

"I love you," I repeated, stepping closer, voice cracking. "Not for the blog. Not for the body. But for the fight in you. The way you clawed your way into peace, and still made room to laugh. The way you survived everything and still had love to give. You're the most honest lie I've ever lived. And I would do it all over again if it meant keeping you alive long enough to love you right."

She sat there, breathing hard, the robe slipping slightly off one shoulder.

"I love you, too," she said, her voice shaking. "But I can't do this."

My heart stopped.

"I want to," she added, tears running down her cheeks now. "But this... all of this..." Her hand swept around the room, that godforsaken wall still looming behind me. "It's too much. It's too deep. Too dark. I don't know how to love someone who became my protector and my predator in the same breath."

I took a step forward, and she backed away.

"I need time," she whispered. "I need space. I need to remember who I was before you walked in with all this chaos disguised as care."

Then she got up, turned, and walked upstairs without another word.

And I stood there, surrounded by pieces of our love story.

I felt loss.

Real, bone-deep, irreversible loss.

The kind you don't recover from.

The kind you only ever experience when you fall in love with a woman like her.

A woman you'd kill for.

And still lose anyway.

22

Rivah

I pulled my clothes back on like armor, like layers could somehow hold me together when I was falling the fuck apart.

My fingers trembled as I shoved my makeup, my charger, my sticky notes—everything I brought to his house—into my tote bag. I could still smell him on the robe I peeled off. Still hearing his voice echoing through the walls like a song I no longer wanted to remember. My skin burned everywhere he had touched me. And my heart... my heart was in shards.

I waited. I gave him time. Time to come up those stairs. Time to stop me. Time to fight for me, but he didn't.

He fucking didn't. And that hurt more than all of it.

I grabbed my purse and walked to the front door with a lump in my throat so big it felt like a fist. But before I could twist the knob, something in me snapped.

I turned back around and walked straight to that damn basement door.

I wanted to see him one more time. To scream. To ask him how the hell he could let me walk away after everything we shared—after everything he did in the name of loving me.

But instead, I planted my feet at the top of the stairs, looked inside, and said loud enough for God and the whole damn gated community to hear:

"Fuck you, Kross!!"

I didn't even wait for a reply. I stormed out the house, and by the time I got to my car, I was shaking. My lungs locked up like they forgot how to breathe, and all I could do was claw at the steering wheel until the world stopped spinning.

I thought about calling Vane, but I couldn't say it all again. Not so soon. Not when my voice was cracked and my spirit was in pieces.

Instead, I let my hands drive me somewhere I hadn't been in years. A place I only went when the world got too heavy and I had no one else to lean on.

I walked slowly between the rows until I reached their headstones.

Randall D. Banks.

Jalisa Renee' Banks.

My parents. My peace.

I dropped to my knees like a little girl again.

The tears hit before the words.

"I don't even know how to tell you what's going on," I whispered, my fingers brushing against the cool stone. "But I fucked up. I opened my heart to a man who loved me so hard he thought killing for me made it okay."

The wind didn't answer. But I felt it. That shift in the air. Like my mama was listening. Like my daddy was still holding me.

"I wanted someone to protect me, and I got it. But not like this," I cried. "I don't know what to do. I love him. God, I love him... but I can't love him like this. I can't lose myself in someone else's damage again."

I hugged my knees, curling into myself as the sky above me darkened, like it felt my pain too.

"I wish y'all were here," I whispered. "I wish I had you to run to... because I don't know if I can do this alone anymore."

And for the first time in years, I felt that ache. The ache of being loved by people who couldn't come back. And the ache of loving someone who might not stay.

I stayed there on the cold grass, knees aching, palms flat on the earth like I was trying to feel their heartbeat beneath the surface.

"I know this ain't the version of me you thought you were raising," I whispered, voice hoarse, almost embarrassed. "But this is who I became when the world kept making me feel like I had to choose between being soft or being safe. Between love or losing myself."

"I've slept with men I didn't love. Talked about them like they were numbers. Rated them like apps. Because somewhere along the way, I realized—men don't break when you fuck them and leave. But women? We shatter. And I got tired of being the one left in pieces. So, I became the one who walked away."

I laughed bitterly through the lump in my throat.

"People call me unhinged. Promiscuous. Too much. But I found power in being the one who gets to choose. They don't know how it feels to live in a world that only values a woman for what she can offer and destroy her when she reclaims it. They made me feel dirty for enjoying sex. For owning it. For not crying when they left, but leaving before they had the chance."

I looked at their names again.

"I never thought anyone could handle me. Tame me. Not because I'm wild, but because I'm fucking honest. I come with grief, trauma, and a smile that hides a thousand stories."

I paused and wiped my eyes with the sleeve of my jacket, then looked up at the dark sky.

"And then he came along..."

The words caught in my throat.

"Kross. With all his secrets and warmth and that mouth that says the right shit at the wrong time. And I let him in. I really let him in. I started thinking maybe I could be soft again. That maybe I didn't have to carry it all by myself."

"But how do I love a man who saw my pain and weaponized it before he ever kissed me? How do I come back from knowing that the one man I let all the way in, got in by breaking every rule I ever set?"

"I don't know how to forgive that. But I also don't know how to stop loving him."

My knees sank deeper into the ground as I folded over, pressing my forehead to my daddy's stone.

"Daddy, you raised me to be strong. To protect myself. But you also taught me how to love loud. And Mama, I know if you were here, you'd tell me that love is messy but it doesn't have to be violent."

"I'm tired of hurting people before they can hurt me. I'm tired of pretending I don't want to be loved just because I'm scared it'll wreck me. But y'all—what do I do when the first man I let truly love me… might be the one who ends me?"

I leaned back, tears streaking my face.

"I don't want to be just a body count."

The sky rumbled softly. Somewhere in the distance, a breeze picked up—soft, like a whisper from another world.

"I just want to be someone's peace," I said.

My soul felt naked. My chest ached like grief had curled up inside it and made a home.

"Let yourself be his peace then," a soft voice floated from behind me.

I jerked slightly, startled. I turned to see a woman, maybe in her late forties, sitting on a bench just a few feet back at another grave. She didn't look at me at first. Her hand was resting on a polished tombstone like she was still holding him. Still anchored by love.

"I'm sorry," I said, trying to compose myself, wiping under my eyes.

She smiled faintly. "Don't be. Tears belong here."

I nodded, swallowing hard.

She stood slowly, walking toward me with grace and a heaviness in her eyes that let me know it wasn't just conversation. This was experience speaking.

She looked at my parents' names, then down at me. "You love him?"

I hesitated.

"I—" My voice cracked. "I don't know what to call it."

"Call it real," she said gently. "Because only something real could break you open like that."

She pointed behind me to the grave she came from.

"That man right there," she said, "he loved me so much, he risked his life for me. Walked into something he should've walked away from just to protect me. And he didn't make it out."

My breath caught.

"I begged him not to go," she continued, "but he just looked at me and said, 'If I go down, it'll be doing something that matters. Something for you.' And I hated him for it when they put him in the ground."

Her voice cracked.

"I hated him for choosing me like that. For leaving me with all the pieces he couldn't put back."

She knelt down beside me, her eyes soft and haunted.

"I didn't show up for him the way he did for me. And every day since, I've wished I could tell him I finally understood. That love like that—messy, chaotic, protective love—it ain't always pretty, but it's rare. It's worth fighting for. Even if it scares you."

I pressed my lips together, blinking back fresh tears.

"I don't know if I can do this," I whispered. "I don't know how to trust someone who's lied to me, even if it was for what he thought was the right reason. He planned everything. Every move. And I let him in, thinking I had all the power. But maybe I never did."

"That's not weakness, baby. That's just the truth," she said, her hand brushing my shoulder gently. "You don't have to have all the answers right now. Love isn't something you figure out overnight. But one thing I know... any man willing to risk his freedom—his life—for yours, is a man your parents would've prayed you'd find."

She stood again, looking down at me like a mother might.

"Go home. Take a shower. Pray. Lay down. But don't you dare let fear or pride cost you something that only shows up once in a lifetime."

"What if I'm not strong enough?"

She gave a sad smile.

"Then let him be strong for you. That's what love is, baby. We carry each other."

She started to walk away but paused one last time, glancing over her shoulder.

"That man sounds like chaos," she said. "But it also sounds like, for once, someone put you first—even if it meant becoming someone you didn't recognize."

23

Rivah

The silence in my house was too loud. Too empty. Too final.

I dropped my keys in the dish by the door, kicked off my shoes, and didn't even bother to turn on the lights. I didn't even realize my lips were moving until the command fell from them, cracked and soft.

"Alexa... play The Commodores."

"Just to Be Close to You" drifted through the speakers, and I damn near dropped to my knees right there.

My daddy's music.

That was the music he always played on days he couldn't carry the weight of her absence anymore. It was their soundtrack. The one he'd dance to by himself in the kitchen, eyes closed, like she was still in his arms.

I was six the first time I caught him doing it. Sixteen when I finally understood why.

I made it to the couch before everything broke loose.

Face first, body limp. I sobbed so hard I thought my lungs would give out. Screams got tangled in the cushions. Tears soaked through the fabric. Every piece of me shattered right there under that low lamp glow and those damn lyrics.

It wasn't just about Kross.

It was years of pain. Years of performing strength like it was my only currency. Of wearing armor so heavy that it bent my back and broke my heart.

And there I was. Alone. Again.

Just like I'd been since the day they buried the only two people who ever really saw me.

"You're gonna be okay," I choked out to myself.

Over and over.

"You're gonna be okay, Rivah. You always are."

My voice shook. My hands trembled against the pillows. But I said it anyway. I had to.

"Get up," I whispered through the tears. "Wash your face. Get your shit together."

I could hear my mama's voice in my head: *"You don't get to lay down and die every time life doesn't love you back."*

And my daddy: *"You're built like a storm, baby girl. Ain't no man gone unmake you."*

The song kept playing.

I imagined them slow-dancing in the middle of my living room.

I imagined them standing behind me now.

I didn't stop crying, but I got up. My knees wobbled, my throat burned, but I stood.

I walked down the hallway, dragging pain behind me like a shadow. My fingertips touched the walls like they could catch me if I collapsed.

And when I stepped into my bedroom, I didn't feel strong.

But I felt... held.

Like maybe—just maybe—I'd survive this, too.

Even if I had to survive it alone.

The bedroom lights flicked on and I damn near jumped out of my damn skin.

"Shit!" I screamed, stumbling back against the wall.

Kross was sitting at the foot of my bed like he'd been there for a minute.

"What the fuck are you doing in here?" My voice cracked. "How the hell did you even get in? This—this is the shit I'm talking about, Kross. This is exactly why—"

"I'm here for you," he said, standing up slowly.

And for the first time in hours, I really looked at him. His eyes. The way they didn't blink or shy away from me. Red-rimmed and heavy like he'd been carrying his own storm all day. The man looked wrecked.

"I could've been in this house months ago," he said quietly. "Do you really think I couldn't? All that tech shit you joke about... you think I couldn't break in with a click? But I didn't. Because I'm not that type of man, Rivah. I didn't want to force my way in. I wanted to be invited."

He took a few steps closer. I didn't move.

"And now I'm telling you... I'm not leaving."

"Kross—"

"No," he snapped, cutting me off with a sharp breath. "You don't get to leave. You don't get to throw all this away because you're scared. I fucked up by not telling you sooner, yes. I crossed lines, yes. But I loved you every step of the way."

Tears burned behind my eyes, but I blinked fast, refusing to let them fall. Not yet.

"You don't get to make all the choices," he said, voice thick with emotion. "You don't get to just walk away when you know damn well we're not done. You said you trusted me. You said you loved me."

"I did—"

"Then act like it!" His voice cracked. "Act like it meant something. Because in everything I've done—even the shit I can't take back—I chose us. You keep choosing survival. I keep choosing you."

I turned away, my chest heaving, my arms folded so tight they were shaking.

He stepped behind me.

"You wanna talk about body counts?" he whispered. "Cool. You're right. That's what it started as. A blog. A list. Men who came and went."

He leaned closer, his voice soft but raw.

"But in your eyes, Rivah... in the way you breathe when you sleep, the way you smile when you think nobody's looking... I don't see a number. I see forever. I don't wanna stop counting the ways I make love to your body. I wanna spend a lifetime keeping score."

I broke.

He pulled me back against his chest before I hit the floor.

"I didn't want to cage you," he whispered, burying his face in my shoulder. "I wanted to carry you. And I knew if I gave you the truth, you'd leave. But even now... after everything... I still believe in us more than I believe in air."

Tears poured down my cheeks. I couldn't stop them.

"I wanted you to come after me," I whispered.

"I did."

"I wanted you to take the choice from me."

"I just did."

He turned me around to face him. No smirk. No games. Just devastation. Just devotion.

"I'm not asking for perfect, Rivah," he said, brushing a tear from my cheek. "I'm asking for a chance. To prove that loving someone doesn't have to hurt."

"I never thought..." My voice cracked. "That anyone could tame me."

"I didn't tame you," he said against my temple. "I loved you wild."

That's what made the tears come harder. Not the words, but the way he said them. Like he meant every vowel. Like his heart had been living in mine since the beginning.

"I'm scared," I finally admitted.

"Me, too."

I pulled back just enough to see his face. Those eyes.

"I be talkin' all that shit," I whispered with a tearful laugh. "But I am really just a big-ass baby with abandonment issues and a smart mouth."

Kross let out a real laugh. "You ain't lying."

"I'm serious, Kross. You're gonna get tired of me."

"Girl, I had five people killed for you. I think I'm in this for the long haul."

I choked on a laugh and smacked his chest. "You cannot joke about that!"

He shrugged. "I can. You're mine now. I wish a motherfucker would look at you too long. You want a body count? Baby, I'll show you one."

"And what if I start wildin' out? You gon' kill me, too?"

"Hell no," he said. "You too fine to kill. I'd just chain you to the bed and feed you grapes until you calm down."

"Unhinged," I whispered, climbing into his lap.

"You knew what it was."

He cupped my face again, eyes searching mine. "We're not perfect, baby. But damn... we're real."

And then he kissed me.

Not like before. Not like a man claiming or seducing. This kiss was relief. Like we had both survived something brutal and needed each other to breathe again. His hands gripped my thighs, dragging me deeper into his lap.

He stood, carrying me effortlessly to the bed as he undressed me.

He hovered over me, bare-chested, breath heavy. "This ain't for fun."

"It never was."

"I ain't just tryna fuck you, Rivah. I'm making love to the woman that shook my whole foundation."

I nodded, chest rising, eyes locked on his.

"And this love," he growled, dragging his mouth down my collarbone, "ain't for play."

His tongue found my nipple while his hand slid down my waist and between my thighs like he knew exactly where to press, exactly how to pull the tension from me.

I arched into him, gasping, my body begging for the punishment of his praise.

"Say it again," I moaned.

"That you're mine?" he whispered against my skin.

"Yes."

He pulled his pants off and gripped my thighs wide, settling between them.

He pushed inside slowly, painfully slow, until I was full—until I swore I could feel him in my throat.

I cried out, grabbing his back, and he growled. **"I'm home."**

He didn't rush. Didn't pound. He pushed. He stroked. He kissed my tears as he moved inside of me like he was writing his name in my body, deep and permanent.

"Let me love you until the pain doesn't fit anymore," he whispered.

"You already are," I cried, wrapping my legs tighter around him.

We cried. We laughed. We moaned into each other like two people who had finally found their ending and weren't ready to let go.

It was baby-making sex, even if no baby was made. Nasty. Slow. Soul-claiming. A remix of pain and pleasure in every thrust.

His pace slowed, but the passion deepened. Every stroke felt intentional.

"Kross..." I whispered, voice trembling.

He didn't stop. Just leaned down, his mouth grazing the shell of my ear.

"No one else," he murmured, voice husky and ragged, "gets access to this."

His hand slid down my thigh, gripping it tighter.

"No one else gets to see you like this. Bent in half, shaking under me, crying from a love you swore you'd never feel again."

He kissed my lips slow, then rough.

"No one else," he growled, "gets to fuck the parts of you they never earned."

I moaned, nails digging into his back, overwhelmed by the way he filled me—physically and spiritually.

"You're more than a body count," he whispered into my mouth. "You're a whole damn story."

His thrusts got deeper, slower, until I could barely hold on to anything but him.

"You're the page I never thought I'd turn. The chapter I re-read in the dark."

I was falling. And this time, I didn't care if I hit the ground.

"I love you, Rivah. Not just this body, but your storm. Your smart-ass mouth. Your secrets. Your survival."

He kissed me like his confession was carved into his tongue.

"I'll spend every night making love to the parts of you that the world tried to break. One stroke at a time, I'll remind you: you're safe now. You're seen. You're mine."

I shattered beneath him.

And as I screamed his name, breathless and undone, I knew—

This wasn't just the end of a chapter.

It was the beginning of everything.

24

Epilogue

"I swear, if one more person comments *'where you at sis?'*, I'm throwing the whole damn WiFi away," I mumbled, pacing through my apartment, the phone pressed to my cheek.

Kross's laugh came through the line, warm and grounding. "They miss you. You built something that meant something."

"Yeah, I know…" I exhaled, walking to the window, heart racing. "It's just—I needed to pour into something else for a while. Into us. Into me."

He went quiet for a second, then said, "You don't owe anyone an explanation, baby."

I smiled. "Maybe not. But they've been on this ride with me since day one. Some of 'em read those posts like therapy. Like war stories they made it out of. I can't just ghost them."

"Then say that," he said, his voice steady. "Say all of it. And I'll be right here."

I bit my lip. "You driving?"

"Yeah, but I'm not far. About two hours out." he replied. "You ready?"

I swallowed. "I think so. Just scared of what they might say."

"You got this," he said. "Say what's on your heart. I'll stay on the phone. Talk it out as you type."

I walked over to my desk, powered up my laptop, and clicked open the blog. My fingers hovered over the keyboard. My heart beat like it was trying to tap out a rhythm my soul already knew.

I clicked *New Post*.
And started typing.

BODY COUNT:
BLOG ENTRY #TheComeback

It's been almost a month since I've posted. Not because I ran out of men to talk about. Not because I got scared. And definitely not because I suddenly became a born-again virgin.

I took a step back... because for the first time in my life, I wanted to choose peace over pain. And honestly, I accidentally let a man turn me into a damn simp. A real-life, sleep-on-the-phone, "you hungry, baby?" kind of simp. Disgusting. Would not recommend. (Okay, maybe just a little.)

I've lived loud for so long. Unapologetic. Unfiltered. Unbothered, but also Unhealed. And sometimes, you have to sit in stillness to hear what your heart's been whispering through the chaos.

And in that stillness, I found something, *someone,* worth slowing down for.

Now, before y'all start throwing rose petals and "aww" reactions under this post, calm down. I still don't believe in fairy tales. I still believe in therapy, boundaries, and checking his phone if your intuition starts itching.

But I also believe in growth.

And the girl who started this blog? She still exists. She's just evolved. Still petty. Still precise. Still not one of them. But now she's sipping wine with her feet on a man's chest who actually deserves to be under them.

So, here's what's new.

We're switching things up.

Body Count will still be unhinged, healing, hilarious, but we're expanding. We're bringing in guests. Yep. Real people. Real experiences. Real warnings. Because one thing about me? I'm a girls' girl. And if that man is a walking red flag, I want you to see him from a zip code away.

These interviews are about to be wild. Therapy session meets tea party meets backseat confessionals.

And yes, I'll still be dragging a few folks in the process. Respectfully. (Kinda.)

As for the man who swept me off my feet?

Don't worry—I'll tell you about him, too.

Might even let y'all meet him. (Spoiler alert: he is fine and crazy. Pray for me.)

I'll be back with my first guest interview *real soon*.

So keep your wigs secured, ladies.

The *Count* has returned.

—Soaked

I exhaled as I clicked post, my heart thudding a little harder than I expected. It felt good to be back. Not just on the blog, but in my skin. In my softness. In my power.

"I love that, baby," Kross said. "That's the version of you I saw before you ever let me in. The one that ain't scared to tell her truth. The one that makes women feel seen and men feel nervous."

I smiled, biting my lip.

"I'm proud of you. You're doing what only the real ones do—healing loud enough to give other people permission to."

"You really gone make me cry, Kross."

"Good. You need to let it out sometimes."

I laughed. "You love me or somethin'?"

"I do. And I'll keep saying it until it never scares you again."

"I'll be there in two hours."

I grinned. "Okay."

"And Rivah?"

"Yeah?"

"Be naked. And ready. 'Cause I got two days' worth of love to make up for."

The line clicked. I stared at the phone, cheeks hot, lips parted.

This man.

Whew.

NETRAANTIONETTE

The doorbell rang just as I was putting my bonnet back on.

I opened the door and saw Niv standing there with a hoodie on and sunglasses like she was lowkey running from TMZ, I busted out laughing.

"Niv! Girl, get your ass in here."

We hugged like we hadn't just texted all night. She smelled like cocoa butter and somebody's son's credit score.

"Come on, I'm taking you to my cave," I said, grabbing her hand and dragging her inside.

The moment she stepped into my blog room—my little messy, moody, candle-lit haven—she spun in a slow circle.

"Oh, bitch. You really got bodies all over the walls. I love it here," she said, eyes wide with mischief. "You got a whole damn Body Count museum. You sure you're not the serial killer, 'cause this giving FBI profiling but make it fine as hell."

I snorted. "It's called art, ma'am."

"It's called sexy," she said, grinning. "I love me a girls' girl."

We both cracked up. Loud. Free. Like we weren't seconds away from documenting confessions that could make or break somebody's man.

"Okay, okay. You ready?" I asked, walking over to my desk and adjusting the mic, my fingers dancing across my laptop keys.

Niv hesitated, biting her lip. "You sure Kross won't know it's me?"

"Girl, no. He knows I'll have guests. Your name in the post is gonna be something ridiculous like *Velveeta Cheese*. Trust me."

She sighed dramatically and flopped into the chair I pulled out for her.

"Kross will be here in like... an hour and a half, so let's wrap this shit up before he starts asking who I was talking to that got me cackling like a villain," I warned.

I handed her a warm cup of my lavender ginger tea and gave her the look.

She narrowed her eyes and said, "This got drugs in it?"

"Just vibes," I smirked. "Don't think. Just drink and spill. I'll type."

She took a sip, exhaled, and I cracked my knuckles.

Body Count: Guest Entry #1 had officially begun.

BODY COUNT:

BLOG ENTRY #TheGuestofAllGuests

You ever watched a man lie straight to your face while his soul tried to sneak out his body? It's my favorite genre of entertainment.

Hi. They call me **Throat Chakra**.

Because every time I open my mouth, a man either loses his mind... or his wallet. Sometimes both.

It's not just what I say—it's how I say it. And yes, if you *read between the lips*, the double meaning is very much intended.

I'm just a woman who's good with her words and quicker with her intuition. And while we're here... let me debunk the myth: You don't have to sleep with a man to make him pay for something. You just need to know how to talk. I've taken "How was your day?" and turned it into rent. You think it's coochie? Nah baby, it's conversation. I've mastered the art of talking a man straight out of his boxer briefs and his wallet.

Men are not that complicated. If you've ever been conned into thinking they are, it's because you haven't graduated from the fine art of Conversation Manipulation 101.

Let me help you.

I'm not saying I've never had to do anything. I'm just saying I've never had to do much. Some women give it up to get flown out. I just ask him how his relationship with his mama is, tilt my head, and next thing you know, we're in Cabo.

Midnight ballerina? Mmm. A walking wet dream with choreography. I move like poetry on stage and make money like men make excuses—consistently. I love what I do. The freedom. The power. The way men turn into Gumby the second I arch my back and touch the floor.

What I do is art. And these men are my materials.

And don't fall for the "men are visual" lie. No. Men are easy. Tell them they're brilliant. Rub their chest once. Act like you believe their crypto coin is gonna take off. Boom. Access granted.

But let's talk about the real gag:

I fell in love. With a hoe.

A hoe who reads books and people.

A hoe who's dangerous with silence and too smart for his own good.

And he thinks I don't know the shit he be doing.

I do.

I just don't react, because my moves would end his whole ecosystem.

You ever hurt a man so bad that his barber starts texting you to check in?

No?

Get your weight up.

I'm not the jealous type. I'm the patient type.

He thinks he's getting away with something?

Baby, I got my lick back two Tuesdays ago. I just came home and made tacos like nothing happened. I got an umbrella for every storm you think you're about to bring.

This entry ain't to bash. It's to let y'all know what's coming. Because while Soaked is out here finding peace and walking in love… I'm still spinning the block in six-inch heels and emotional detachment. This ain't your average love story.

Let this be your warning:

I talk too pretty to beg.

I move too smart to get played.

And if I ever do cry, just know I'm either on my period or planning your funeral.

The next entry might just ruin someone's life.

Stay tuned.

– **Throat Chakra**
THE END

Netra's Notebook

Netra Antionette writes with a heart rooted in Black stories that honor softness, strength, survival, and above all, our power to choose love on our own terms. Whether it's the ache of generational wounds or the joy of hard-earned healing, her stories are a celebration of resilience, a reclamation of tenderness, and a mirror for the kind of love Black women—and all those who've ever been told they're too much or not enough—deserve. Netra Antoinette holds a master's in business administration; a degree she pursued to support her creative vision to navigate the literary world with intention. When she's not writing, she's embracing her most cherished role: being a wife and mother, grounding her work in the same love and resilience she writes about.

Want more?

Visit her website at www.netraantionette.com to shop signed books, bundles, and exclusive goodies.

Join Netra's Notebook

https://www.facebook.com/share/g/1Y7ENSNY21/?mibextid=wwXIfr

Made in the USA
Coppell, TX
17 February 2026

72031587R10108